# THAT FRUIT IS MINE!

## ANUSKA ALLEPUZ

Albert Whitman & Company

Chicago, Illinois

Deep in the heart of the jungle,
lived five elephants.

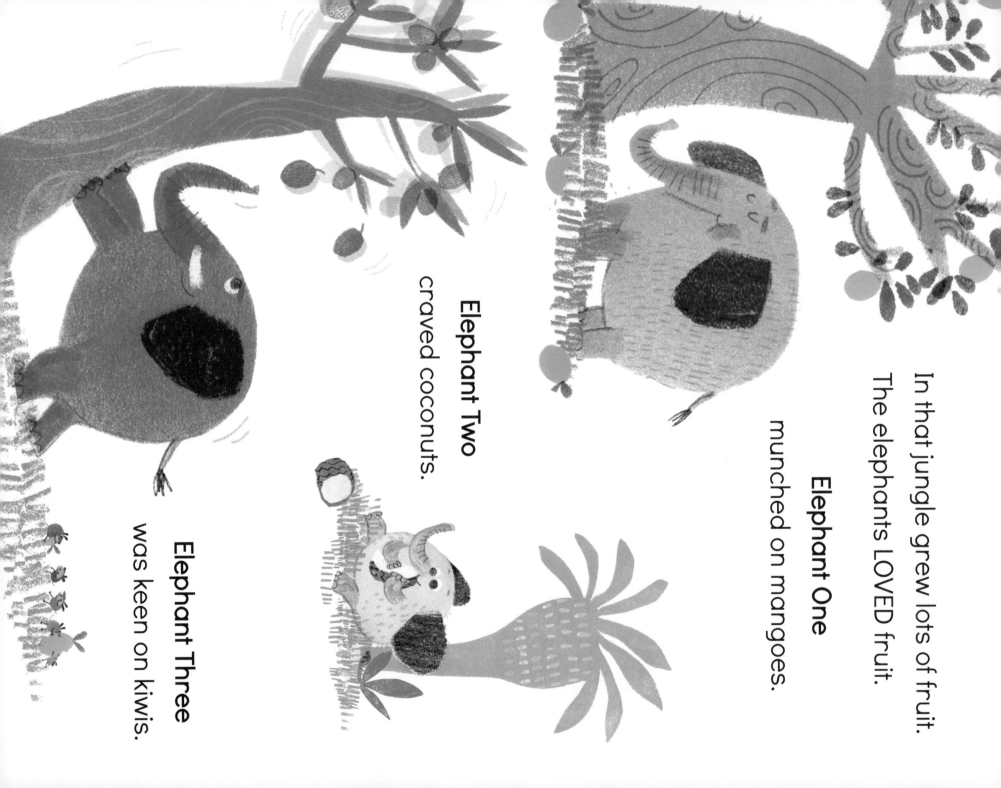

In that jungle grew lots of fruit.
The elephants LOVED fruit.

**Elephant One**
munched on mangoes.

**Elephant Two**
craved coconuts.

**Elephant Three**
was keen on kiwis.

Elephant Four
banqueted on bananas.

And Elephant Five
preferred pineapples.

But one day, deep, *deep* in the heart
of the jungle, the elephants discovered
a new tree. A very TALL, new tree.

And on that very tall tree was the MOST delicious-looking exotic fruit the elephants had ever seen.

EVERYONE wanted to eat it.

Hey, look at THAT!

# "MINE!"

cried Elephant One.
"That fruit is MINE!"

She KNEW that she could reach it.
She *huffed* and she *puffed*
with all her might...

One,
two,
three,
four,
five.
Up,
up,
up!

# PFFFT!

The fruit didn't move an itty-bitty inch.

Heave
ho!
One,
two,
three,
four,
five.
Up,
up,
up!

"MINE!"
said Elephant Two.
"That fruit is MINE!"

Keep stretching!

She KNEW that she had a very smart idea. She could already taste that sweet, sweet fruit...

Look! A humongous bug!

HMPH!

Well, maybe her idea needed a little more work.

# "MINE!"

shouted Elephant Three.

"That fruit is MINE!"

He KNEW that he was cleverer

than Elephant One and Elephant Two.

So, with a he-e-e-eave

and a stre-e-e-etch

he started to climb...

Not far
to go
now!
One,
two,
three,
four,
five.
Up,
up,
up!

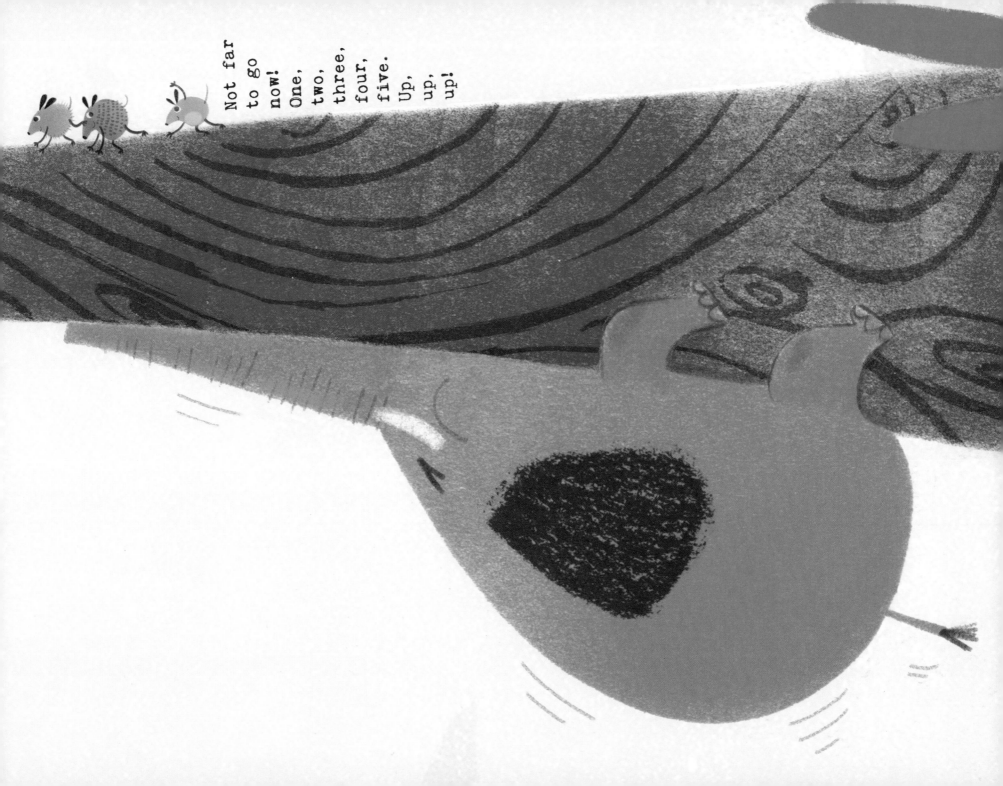

# OOF!

He didn't get very far at all.

I can almost reeeeeeach!

The elephants were getting VERY impatient and VERY hungry! Elephant Four decided to just run at the tree as fast as he could.

"MINE!"

said the elephants, all at once.

But at that very moment...

the delicious-looking exotic fruit began...

to MOVE!

Oops. I beg your pardon!

Now the delicious-looking exotic fruit belonged
to the five mice, who carried it...TOGETHER!

"This fruit is OURS!" the five mice said.

The elephants looked on, astonished.

"OURS?"

said the elephants.

Hooray!
We've got
the fruit!

"OURS!"

said the elephants, all at once.

"Why didn't we think of that!?"

Huff!

*Puff!*

"OURS!"

Huff!

Huff!

He-e-e-eave!

# "OURS!"

Stre-e-e-etch!

"This fruit is OURS!"

And that's how, deep, _deep_ in the heart
of the jungle, the elephants finally got
their delicious-looking exotic fruit.

"Weren't there
five of us?"

"OURS!"

Thank you most of all to Mom and my brother Alberto.

Thank you to Martin Salisbury, Alexis Deacon, Anne-Louise Jones, Maria Tunney, and Helen Mackenzie-Smith.

Thank you all for making it possible for me to create this book, my first picture book!

Library of Congress Cataloging-in-Publication data is on file with the publisher.

First published in 2018 by Walker Books Ltd. Text and illustrations copyright © Anuska Allepuz.
Published in 2018 by Albert Whitman & Company
ISBN 978-0-8075-7894-0

Printed in China
10 9 8 7 6 5 4 3 2 1 RRD 22 21 20 19 18 17

Cover design by Morgan Beck

For more information about Albert Whitman & Company,
visit our website at www.albertwhitman.com.

# Learn to Play Guitar with Metallica
## Volume 2

### By Toby Wine

Recording Credits: Toby Wine, Guitar

Photo by Mark Leialoha

Cherry Lane Music Company
Educational Director/Project Supervisor: Susan Poliniak
Director of Publications: Mark Phillips
Manager of Publications: Gabrielle Fastman

ISBN-13: 978-1-57560-865-5
ISBN-10: 1-57560-865-0

*Visit our website at www.cherrylane.com*

# CONTENTS

# INTRODUCTION

With this book, we pick up where we left off in *Learn to Play Guitar with Metallica*, mastering our instrument by studying the music of the most influential and enduring metal band of the last 20 years. Instead of trudging our way through boring exercises and endless patterns to learn technique, we'll use excerpts from Metallica's music to make the same points and gain the same skills—and we'll have fun doing it! While many of the topics here will be familiar to readers of that first volume, the aim now is to explore in greater detail the techniques involved in the execution of this difficult music, and to tackle the more advanced passages and demanding moments in the Metallica canon.

Note: Track 1 contains tuning pitches.

# ABOUT THE AUTHOR

Toby Wine was born and raised in New York City and studied guitar and composition at the Manhattan School of Music. As a teenager, he led his own thrash and hardcore band, Infantile Disorder, attended CBGB's Sunday matinees religiously, wrote for fanzines covering the scene, and swapped demo and concert tapes with punk and metal bands from around the world. He has worked as both a bandleader and a sideman in many of the tri-state area's most prestigious rooms. His compositions and arrangements can be found in the repertoires of a variety of vocal and instrumental performers, and can be heard on recordings by Philip Harper (*Soulful Sin* and *The Thirteenth Moon*; Muse Records), Ari Ambrose (*Early Song*; Steeplechase), and Ian Hendrickson Smith (*Up in Smoke*; Sharp Nine). He has also done orchestration and score preparation work for the avant-garde icon Ornette Coleman and served as band librarian for the Carnegie Hall Jazz Band. When not in the studio or teaching privately, he can be heard around the tri-state area performing with various jazz bands and the R&B/salsa collective Melee. Toby is the author of *The Art of Texas Blues*, *Metallica Under the Microscope*, *Zakk Wylde Legendary Licks*, and numerous other Cherry Lane titles.

# ACKNOWLEDGMENTS

My most heartfelt thanks to my editor, Susan Poliniak, and to John, Mark, Gabi, and the rest of the great staff at Cherry Lane. Thanks also to Lissette, Bibi, Bob, Jack, Taddy Mack, Gebb, Sam, Mover, Humph, Kenny, Manny (R.I.P.), Ritchie Aprile, and the rest of my great friends and teachers. Extra special love and gratitude to my parents, Rosemary and Jerry.

# CHAPTER 1

## A Music-Reading Refresher Course

Before we dive into the headbanging lessons found in Metallica's music, let's quickly review some fundamentals of reading music in standard notation (don't worry, the examples in this book include tablature as well).

Guitarists read almost exclusively in *treble clef*, shown in the diagram below on the farthest left margin. In treble clef, from bottom to top, the horizontal lines represent the pitches E, G, B, D, and F, and the spaces in between represent the pitches F, A, C, and E.

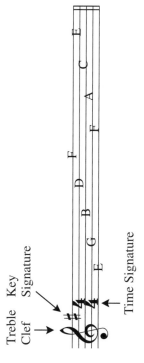

The *key signature* is found immediately to the right of the clef. This might be any number of sharp (♯) or flat (♭) signs; it tells you which key you are in and which specific pitches are to be raised or lowered (unless the piece is in C major or A minor, in which case no sharps or flats appear in the key signature). The example has a key signature that contains one sharp, F♯, which indicates the key of G major or E minor, and that all Fs should be raised one half step. If the music calls for an F♮, it will be indicated for a note, and all Fs will then remain "naturalized" for the duration of that measure unless another accidental comes along to change the situation. If another F♮ is needed in the measure that follows, it will be indicated again, while a sharp sign will be supplied as a "courtesy" if you are to return to the F♯ of the key signature.

It may take a while to memorize which key is indicated by which number of sharps or flats, so here's a logical system to use: Begin with the key of C major, which has no *accidentals* (sharps, flats, or naturals). Flat keys move through the *cycle of 4ths*, so go up a perfect 4th interval from C major (to F major) to find the key that contains one flat. Go up another 4th to B♭ major, and you'll have two flats. Another 4th up takes you to E♭ major, which has three, and so on (this works for minor keys, too). Sharp keys move through the *cycle of 5ths*. Starting once again at C major, go up a perfect 5th to G major (one sharp), another to D major (two sharps), and another to A major (three sharps), etc. (again, this also works for minor keys). In time you'll come to remember which key has which number of sharps or flats, particularly those keys you encounter most frequently.

Immediately to the right of the key signature is the *time signature*. The top number in the fraction indicates the number of beats in each measure, and the bottom number indicates the rhythmic value of one beat. A key signature of 4/4 indicates four quarter notes in each measure, while 6/8 indicates six eighth notes; 4/4 is by far the most common time signature, but Metallica frequently shifts time signatures during the course of a song. Examples that include shifts of this type will be examined and explained in detail later on.

The diagram below shows the location of the six open-string notes of the guitar as they appear on the staff. Note that the open E and A strings lie below the staff, so they are placed on *ledger lines*, additional little horizontal lines that effectively expand the staff's range. Ledger lines are also used above the staff for notes too high to fit within its confines.

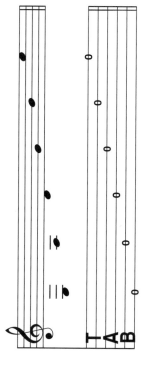

Note that the above example also includes a *tablature staff*, or *tab*. The lines indicate the six strings of the guitar, and the numbers on them indicate the fretting.

Now let's refresh our knowledge of rhythmic values. The following diagram shows common rhythms, their names, and their musical lengths in 4/4 time.

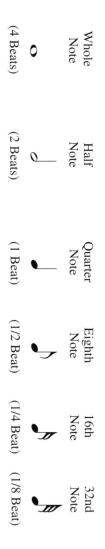

| Whole Note | Half Note | Quarter Note | Eighth Note | 16th Note | 32nd Note |
|---|---|---|---|---|---|
| (4 Beats) | (2 Beats) | (1 Beat) | (1/2 Beat) | (1/4 Beat) | (1/8 Beat) |

*Dots* are often added immediately to the right of a given notehead, increasing that note's length by 50%. A dotted quarter note lasts for three eighth notes (one and a half quarter notes), while a dotted half note lasts for three quarter notes (one and a half half notes). A *tie* connecting two notes indicates that only the first is to be played, and it will last the duration of both rhythms combined. In the example below, the first dotted half note lasts from beats 1 to 3, while the quarter note that follows falls on beat 4 and is held over to beat 1 of the next measure. The second dotted half note falls on beat 2 of that measure and lasts till its end.

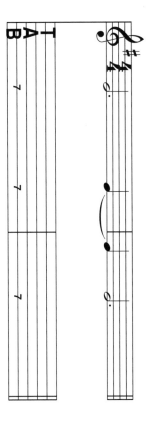

Finally, let's review the various rest symbols. As you probably know by now, a rest tells you not to play—but for how long?

| Whole Rest | Half Rest | Quarter Rest | Eighth Rest | 16th Rest | 32nd Rest |
|---|---|---|---|---|---|
| (4 Beats) | (2 Beats) | (1 Beat) | (1/2 Beat) | (1/4 Beat) | (1/8 Beat) |

Rests can be dotted, but they are never tied.

This little review is by no means comprehensive, but it isn't intended to be. By all means pursue a greater knowledge of, and facility with, standard notation by sight-reading daily and studying one of the many excellent books available on the subject. Now, however, it's time to get shredding!

# CHAPTER 2

## Single-Note Playing and Alternate Picking

Let's begin (or should I say, resume?) our education one note at a time with some of Metallica's best single-note lines. It would seem that single-note playing might be easier to manage than riffs made up of *double stops* (two notes played at once) or chords, but this often isn't the case; single-note licks and riffs are often highly ornate, complex, and fast. Let's tackle a handful of passages taken from the band's songs that can be used to help build up your single-note prowess.

The default mode for your picking hand in these situations (and in most chordal passages, as well) is *alternate picking*, in which you play alternating downstroke and upstrokes. There are instances in which you might be called upon to play a passage with consecutive downstrokes, but this technique, which supplies an element of added "heaviness," is limited by the fact that you just can't do repeated downstrokes all that quickly. A lightning fast single-note line would be nearly impossible without employing alternate picking, so it behooves you to have this important technique down cold. A great way to start working on it is to take a passage like the one below, from the opening moments of "Seek and Destroy," and loop it around on itself indefinitely, using a metronome to set as slow a pace as you need to execute the line perfectly.

## "Seek & Destroy" Verse Riff from *Kill 'Em All*

TRACK 02

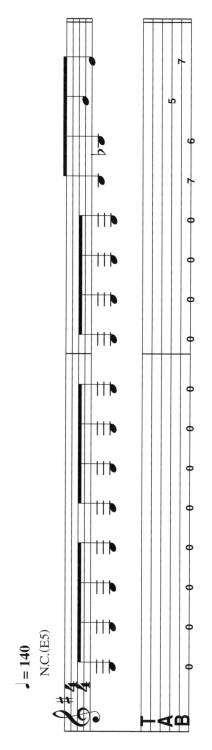

Try gripping the pick between your thumb and forefinger. "Choke up" on it so that there's very little pick actually showing; it's simply easier to control and hold on to this way. Also, try keeping your thumb's knuckle joint unbent—another way to improve pick control. By keeping the tip of the pick pointed roughly in towards your body, you can achieve a more consistent tone and attack than if you were to hit the strings at an angle. Try a pick on the heavier side as well; a lighter pick may bend quite a bit and is usually too "floppy" for clean single-note playing or heavy riffing. Perhaps most important is that you should find a way to anchor your picking hand so that it's not just floating freely above the strings the way that it does when it strums full chords. Many players rest the bottom of the palm lightly on the bridge just at the point where the strings reach the saddles, allowing for easy on-and-off palm-muting, while others place their pinky and ring fingertips on the guitar's pickguard, or wrap their pinky around the volume knob. This is a highly individual choice and one that should be made with an awareness of the physical dimensions of one's own hands and instrument. Regardless, achieving a strong picking technique without anchoring the hand in some way is difficult to say the least, so give it a shot if you're not already doing it. Finally, strive for a minimum of motion in the picking hand. You should be making small, contained movements, so watch yourself closely and eliminate any excess flailing about that may inhibit your speed.

Try applying these principles to the single-note lines that follow, beginning with this excerpt from "Disposable Heroes" (*Master of Puppets*) that doesn't involve the fretting hand at all, allowing you to concentrate exclusively on your alternate picking technique.

## "Disposable Heroes" Verse Riff from *Master of Puppets*

TRACK 03

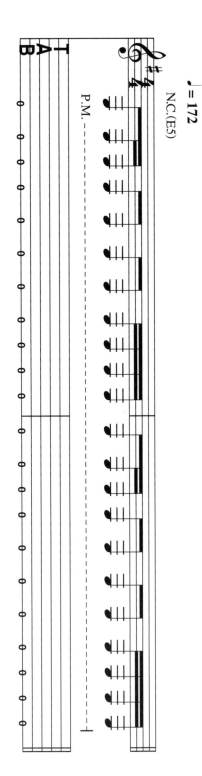

You may have noticed the "P.M." marking on the example above, indicating the common palm-muting technique mentioned earlier. If you already have your picking hand anchored to your guitar's bridge, this is merely the simple task of moving the hand forward (towards the neck) a few fractions of an inch to rest it lightly on the strings, creating a slightly muffled sound that doesn't obscure the actual pitches you're playing. The palm mute is an important technique that Metallica employs frequently to add accents and textural variety to riffs and licks; we'll discuss it further later on. For now, take a stab at this single-note line from "Fixxxer." Don't miss the hammer-on from D to E that begins the phrase, or the little micro-bend (less than a half step) later in the measure.

## "Fixxxer" Intro Riff from *ReLoad*

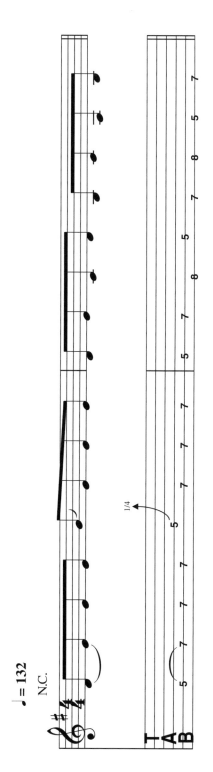

Words and Music by James Hetfield, Lars Ulrich and Kirk Hammett
Copyright © 1997 Creeping Death Music (ASCAP)
International Copyright Secured   All Rights Reserved

Slow and steady is the name of the game when building technical prowess on your instrument. Don't worry about how fast Metallica plays a given line on an album—play it as slowly as you need to in order to execute it flawlessly. Use a metronome to ensure perfect time and gauge your progress by increasing the speed in small increments every other day or so (do not speed up until you can really play the line with ease!). Repeat the excerpt over and over to build muscle memory and coordination between picking and fingering hands. Think of Michael Jordan shooting 5,000 jumpshots a day and you'll get the idea!

This next example is taken from "The Call of Ktulu" and features a repeated D-string phrase that "pivots" off of ascending notes on the A string. Play this one strictly in 7th position; i.e., all notes on the 7th fret should be played with the index finger, use your middle finger for those on the 8th, ring finger for 9th-fret notes, and pinky for those on the 10th.

This is the first of many tracks on the CD that includes a "play-along." For these, the right channel contains the part you should play, and the left channel contains another guitar part you can play along to.

# "The Call of Ktulu" Single-Note Line from *Ride the Lightning*

TRACK 05

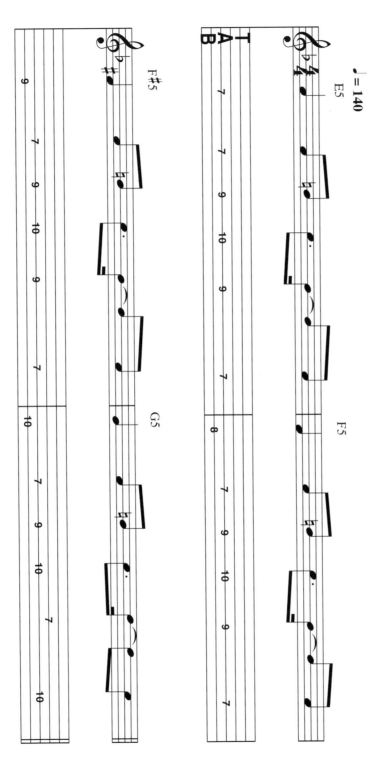

Words and Music by James Hetfield, Lars Ulrich, Clifford Burton and David Mustaine
Copyright © 1984 Creeping Death Music (ASCAP)
International Copyright Secured   All Rights Reserved

Next up is an interesting phrase from the brutal "Battery." This one is in 4th position, requiring you to begin the line with your pinky. Reach down with your index finger to the A string's 3rd fret in measure 2, and then use your ring finger to slide up from D to E (don't pick the E). Pull off from your 3rd to your 1st finger to execute the triplet in measure 3, and observe the palm-mute indications, which give the line shape and carefully chosen accents.

## "Battery" Interlude Lick from *Master of Puppets*

**TRACK 06**

Let's move on to a triplet-based line taken from "For Whom the Bell Tolls," played entirely in 7th position. This one is pretty straightforward but it makes a nice alternate picking exercise as it moves continuously between the B and G strings and contains no rests. It seems to lay better when begun with an upstroke of the pick, so that when you jump down to the G string you hit it with a downstroke.

## "For Whom the Bell Tolls" Intro Lick from *Ride the Lightning*

**TRACK 07**

11

Let's wrap up our discussion of single-note lines and alternate picking with a return to "Seek & Destroy." This time it's the lick that begins the tune, and it's a bit harder by virtue of its string-skipping, hammer-ons, and tied notes. Keep in mind that any challenging line should be isolated, slowed down, and repeated endlessly until your technique catches up with the demands placed upon it.

## "Seek & Destroy" Intro Lick from *Kill 'Em All*

TRACK 08

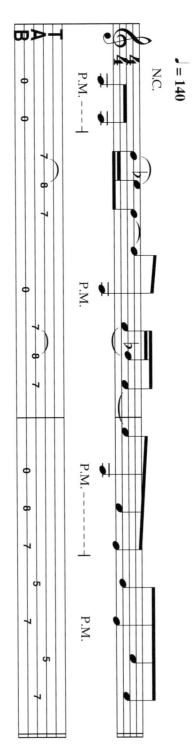

# CHAPTER 3

## Power Chords

*Power chords*, which pair a root with a second pitch a 5th above (and sometimes with a third note an octave above the root), are the brick and mortar of Metallica's riff-based songs. If you worked your way through the first volume in this series, or have any experience with metal or hard rock guitar, the power chord should be familiar to you. However, not all power chords are created equally.

Let's begin with the following excerpt from "Master of Puppets." Because of its medium tempo, the passage can be played predominantly with downstrokes to give it added heft. In fact, the only place you'll need to use alternate picking is for the two quick C#s at the end of the first measure. Fret the power chords with your index and ring fingers, moving smoothly, but make each chord distinct; you don't want to hear any sliding here. Add in the palm muting throughout and you've got a nice, crunchy riff with serious head-banging drive.

## "Master of Puppets" Interlude Riff from *Master of Puppets*

TRACK 09

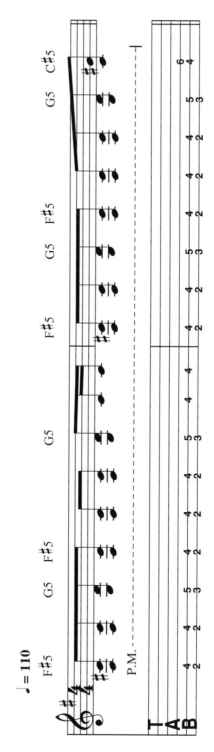

Words and Music by James Hetfield, Lars Ulrich, Kirk Hammett and Cliff Burton
Copyright © 1986 Creeping Death Music (ASCAP)
International Copyright Secured   All Rights Reserved

This simple riff from "The Four Horsemen" is strongly reminiscent of earlier, highly influential bands like Black Sabbath and, to a lesser extent, Iron Maiden. It wasn't long before the band got away from this style by ratcheting up their speed and intensity to a high degree. Nonetheless, it contains a technique found throughout the band's work—the alternating of single-string playing with power chord hits in a higher register. You'll need to resume your alternate picking approach here, as the palm-muted triplets in the example just don't sound right if played with all downstrokes. The various power chords here should, though, be played with all downstrokes, as they require extra emphasis. Also, check out the first power chord in the example's final measure. It's a C5 chord in which the 5th is doubled an octave below, giving us a three-note chord in inversion so that the root isn't the lowest pitch. These pop up on occasion but aren't as common as the three-note power chord in which the root is doubled an octave higher.

## "The Four Horsemen" Verse Riff from *Kill 'Em All*

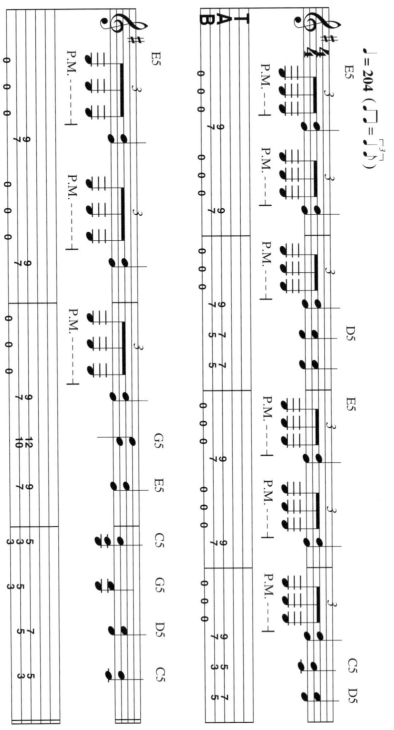

Words and Music by James Hetfield, Lars Ulrich and Dave Mustaine
Copyright © 1983 Creeping Death Music (ASCAP)
International Copyright Secured  All Rights Reserved

Let's stay with the early stuff a bit longer. This next example from "Motorbreath" is a bit tougher in that there's a lot of moving around on the two lowest strings; it's also pretty damn fast. Don't even try to play it at full tempo until you can play it perfectly at a much slower pace—this means perfect time, smooth transitions from chord to chord, good tone, and any added details, such as the palm muting involved here. Loop it around on itself until you're ready to ratchet up the speed—the same practice method you should be applying to all of the examples in the book. This one also presents a picking challenge, in that everything should be played with downstrokes—even at this fast tempo—except the 16th note figures, which should be alternate picked. When you pick up the pace after familiarizing yourself with this riff, be careful not to slide around too much; you want to hear crisp, distinct power chords clearly separated from each other.

## "Motorbreath" Verse Riff from *Kill 'Em All*

**TRACK 11**

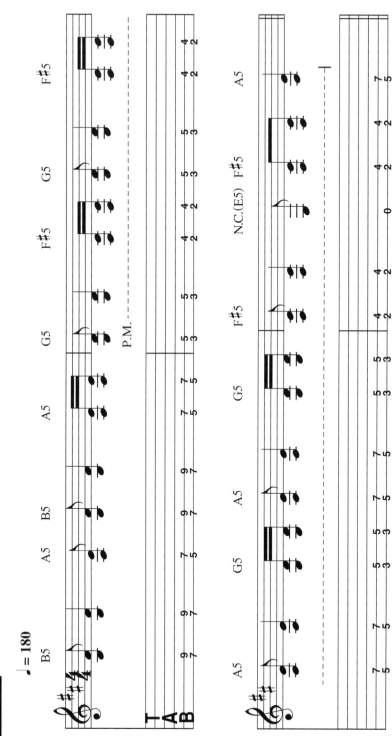

Words and Music by James Hetfield
Copyright © 1983 Creeping Death Music (ASCAP)
International Copyright Secured   All Rights Reserved

Now let's jump ahead to "The House Jack Built." Be sure to tune down each of your strings one half step if you're going to play along with the recording. This is a fairly easy riff taken from the song's pre-chorus section but it introduces a new technique—the sliding power chord. During each of the three slides included here, pick only the first power chord and slide your fretting hand up. The moderate tempo allows for all downstrokes, while the on-and-off palm muting gives the riff accent and a nice dynamic contour.

# "The House Jack Built" Pre-Chorus Riff from *Load*

TRACK 12

Tune down 1/2 step:
(low to high) Eb-Ab-Db-Gb-Bb-Eb

♩ = 100
N.C.

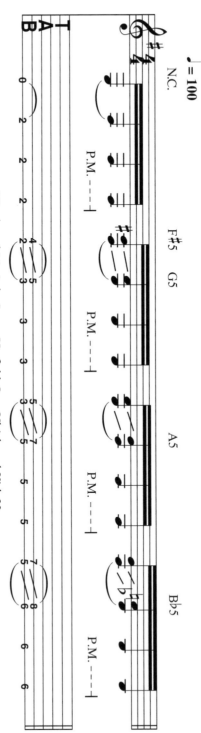

# "Battery" Coda Riff from *Master of Puppets*

TRACK 13

In this riff from the coda to "Battery," the band lays down a sequence of thunderously accented blasts—which makes this an excellent exercise for mastering shifting three-note power chords. Here we find the species mentioned earlier, in which the root is doubled an octave higher. In each case, the lowest note should be played with the index finger while the two pitches above should be played with a ring-finger barre. And, of course, it's all downstrokes from start to finish.

♩ = 190

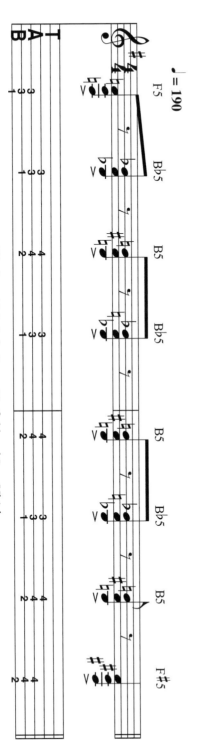

Here's another riff that includes three-note power chords. Once again, the band is tuned down a half step, so don't forget to make the requisite adjustment if you want to play along. This is a typical Metallica passage in that it includes precisely placed palm-mutes and accents—don't omit these details, as they're essential to getting an authentic sound. The 16 eighth notes here are divided by the mutes into groupings of three and four notes, creating an over-the-bar-line feeling frequently encountered in the band's writing. You can use all downstrokes for this one.

## "Wasting My Hate" Ending Riff from *Load*

Tune down 1/2 step:
(low to high) Eb-Ab-Db-Gb-Bb-Eb

♩ = 148

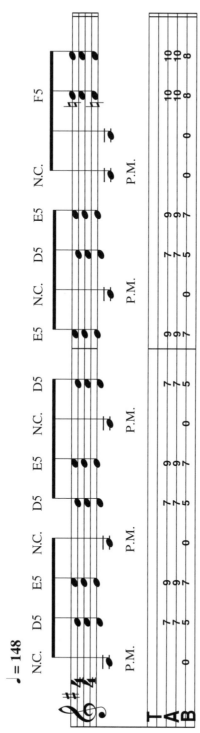

Words and Music by James Hetfield, Lars Ulrich and Kirk Hammett
Copyright © 1996 Creeping Death Music (ASCAP)
International Copyright Secured   All Rights Reserved

Next up, here's the pre-chorus riff from the title track of *...And Justice for All*, which includes both three-note power chords and slides. Be sure to distinguish between the standard slides and the grace-note slides in the second measure. The latter should take up virtually no time at all, serving as quick little approaches from below to the target G5 chords—pick only the grace-note chord and slide it up quickly to the G5 "target."

## "*...And Justice for All*" Pre-Chorus Riff from *...And Justice for All*

♩ = 168

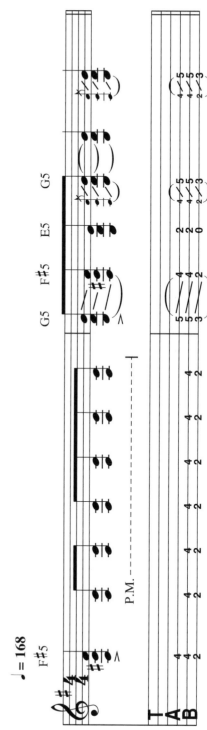

Words and Music by James Hetfield, Lars Ulrich and Kirk Hammett
Copyright © 1988 Creeping Death Music (ASCAP)
International Copyright Secured   All Rights Reserved

Finally, take a look at this riff from the intro to "Harvester of Sorrow." The slow tempo allows for downstrokes exclusively, turning the passage into an ultra-heavy mosh-pit catalyst. This one really has it all, including three-note power chords, slides, mutes, and accents. Be sure to contrast the sliding chords with the clearly delineated chords—there's a major difference in both sound and feel.

# "Harvester of Sorrow" Intro Riff from ...And Justice for All

Words and Music by James Hetfield and Lars Ulrich
Copyright © 1988 Creeping Death Music (ASCAP)
International Copyright Secured   All Rights Reserved

TRACK 16

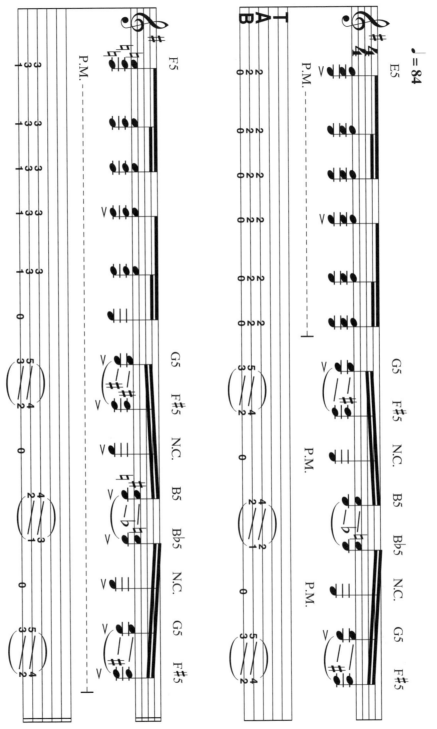

# CHAPTER 4

## Triads and Other Chords

There's a good reason power chords are vastly more prevalent in Metallica's music than full chords that include 3rds, 7ths, and the like: The richer harmonies have a tendency to quickly turn to mud when played through a wall of amps cranked to ear-splitting volumes! That said, the band's writing has evolved over the last two decades, and has come to include moments of dynamic shift that reach into quieter though no less intense passages, in which more complex chord voicings play a part. In the following examples, we'll look at some of the ways the band has incorporated full chords into their writing and the various techniques required to play these parts correctly. Bear in mind that this chapter isn't remotely comprehensive, and that a strong knowledge of, and facility with, chord playing is essential for any guitarist with serious aspirations.

Let's begin with the following excerpt from "Low Man's Lyric" in 3/4 time. One way that chords can be played is with *arpeggios*, in which the chord's individual notes are played in succession, rather than all at once as in a strumming part. Often, arpeggio parts are played with the fingers, but we'll use alternate picking for this one beginning on A minor. In the second measure, merely remove your index finger from the B string to create the Amsus2 chord (essentially, an A minor chord with an added second scale degree), and then shift down to F in measure 3. Use your index, ring, and pinky fingers on the low E, A, and D strings, respectively, while your middle finger moves on and off the G string as indicated. Don't forget to tune all six strings down one half step if you're going to play along with the recording. Also, note that the music may be marked with different chords to coincide with what the band is doing, so you need to rely on what the notes spell as opposed to the chords listed—and this goes for *any* piece of music by *any* rock band.

## "Low Man's Lyric" Bridge Riff from *ReLoad*

**TRACK 17**

Tune down 1/2 step:
(low to high) E♭–A♭–D♭–G♭–B♭–E♭

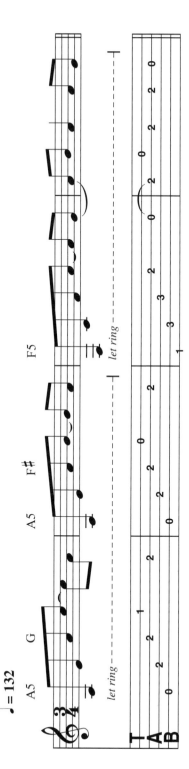

In the intro to "The Unforgiven II," a melody line in octaves is accompanied by the following open-position chord figure—a model of simplicity. Each of these voicings should be extremely familiar to anyone whose playing experience is anything more than nominal. Merely move between Am, C, G, and E chords while strumming each twice with a downstroke of the pick in a quarter note rhythm (we're also back to our "half step down" tuning here). Notice that the A string isn't played during the G chords in measure 2; flatten your middle finger slightly on the 3rd fret of the low E string to mute that open string.

## "The Unforgiven II" Intro Chords from *ReLoad*

TRACK 18

Tune down 1/2 step:
(low to high) Eb-Ab-Db-Gb-Bb-Eb

♩ = 68

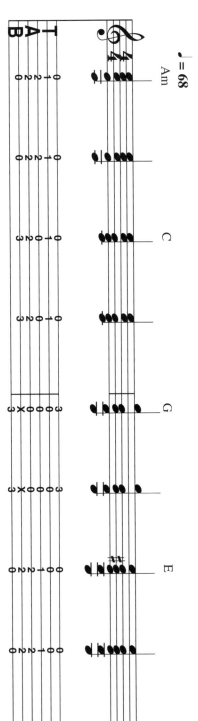

Words and Music by James Hetfield, Lars Ulrich and Kirk Hammett
Copyright © 1997 Creeping Death Music (ASCAP)
International Copyright Secured   All Rights Reserved

The second instrumental interlude in "…And Justice for All" is based on the figure below, a nice mix of single notes, power chords, open-position chords, and barre chords. It also includes a shift from 4/4 to 2/4 and then back again; count out the quarter note beats if there's any confusion as to how the part should sound (don't worry, there will be more on time signature shifts in the next chapter). Two other facets of this part merit close attention. First, you'll need to play F, A, and B♭ barre chords, flattening your index finger across all six strings in addition to your other three fret-hand fingers on the A, D, and G strings. If barre chords are new to you, stop for a moment as you play each and make sure that each note in the chord rings clear—the pressure needed to play a barre chord cleanly may take some time. There are also picking issues to be considered. Try playing the figure with all downstrokes except for the 16th note groupings in the first and third measures—try these with quick down-up alternate pick attacks. This isn't set in stone, and you may find another picking variation more comfortable to you, but the one described above allows for ease of playability and the appropriate heaviness called for by the riff. Note that we're back in standard tuning here.

# "…And Justice for All" Second Interlude from …And Justice for All

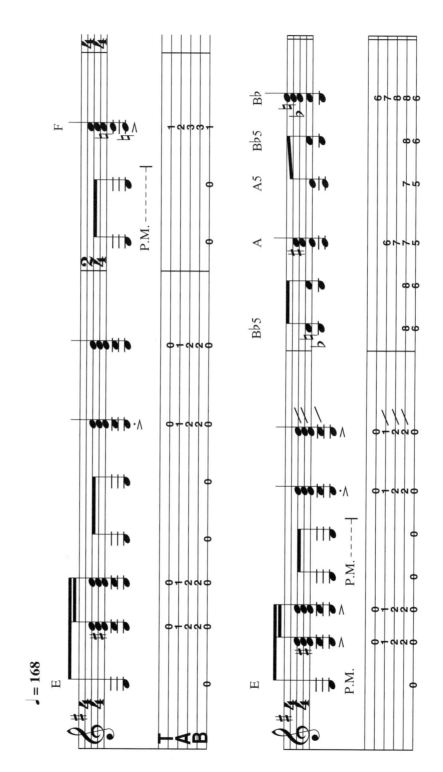

Words and Music by James Hetfield, Lars Ulrich and Kirk Hammett
Copyright © 1988 Creeping Death Music (ASCAP)
International Copyright Secured   All Rights Reserved

Finally, let's look at the intro to "Where the Wild Things Are," which mixes strummed chords with an interesting arpeggio figure, and also includes a shift from 2/4 to 4/4. The opening Em chord is easy; play the Cmaj7 chord that follows with your middle finger on the A string (3rd fret) and index finger on the D string (2nd fret). This fingering allows you to stay in place, letting the indicated strings ring as you move on to the arpeggios and add your ring finger to the G string. Merely move it down from the 4th to the 3rd fret to create the C7 chord, and then lift it off entirely for the C triad at the end of measures. The squiggly line to the left of the Em chords indicate a slightly "dragged" downstroke of the pick, which allows for a very small, barely audible delineation of the chord's individual notes. Contrast this with a swift downstroke in which all notes are heard at once, and you'll see that the effect is significantly different. And don't forget to tune down a half step again for play-along purposes!

## "Where the Wild Things Are" Intro from ReLoad

TRACK 20

Tune down 1/2 step:
(low to high) E♭–A♭–D♭–G♭–B♭–E♭

♩ = 92

Em    Cmaj7    C7    C    N.C.

*let ring throughout*

Em    Cmaj7    C7    C    N.C.

# CHAPTER 5

## Time Signature Shifts and Metric Modulations

From the beginning, Metallica's compositions have featured shifts of time signature and meter that add yet another demanding aspect to their music. In this section, we'll examine some of those moments and look at how to count and feel through them.

This example from the intro to "...And Justice for All" shifts from 4/4 to 2/4 and then back again to 4/4. Remember that in any time signature, the top number represents the number of beats in a measure, while the lower figure indicates the rhythmic value of one beat. The example below is pretty simple to count and follow; just say (or tap) "1-2-3-4/1-2-3-4/1-2/1-2-3-4."

## "...And Justice for All" Intro Riff from *...And Justice for All*

**TRACK 21**

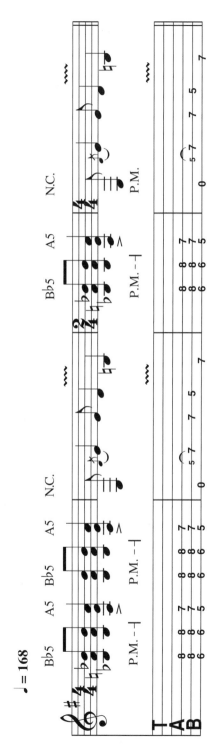

In the following excerpt the music shifts from 4/4 to 3/4. While this shift may seem disorienting at first, close examination of the line reveals a similarity—the last quarter note of the 4/4 measures is "lopped off" for the 3/4 measures. Try singing or tapping out the quarter note rhythms of the line slowly without your guitar before trying to play it. Be sure that you understand how to count and "feel" the time signature shift and that you always know where beat 1 is. They just get harder from here, so you'll want to get this example down, and then do this with each of the examples that follow.

## "Disposable Heroes" Pre-Chorus Riff from *Master of Puppets*

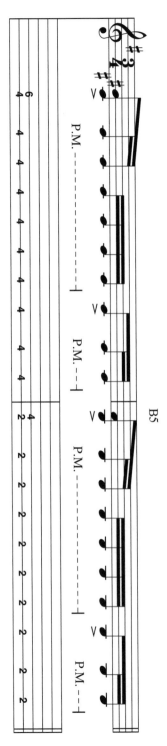

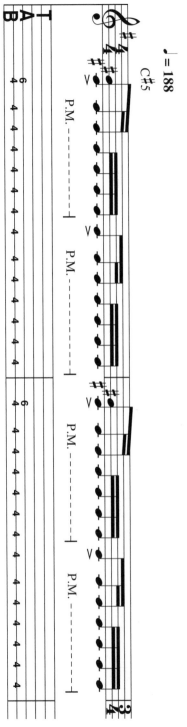

Words and Music by James Hetfield, Lars Ulrich and Kirk Hammett
Copyright © 1986 Creeping Death Music (ASCAP)
International Copyright Secured   All Rights Reserved

Let's look at a riff from "Dyers Eve" that bounces back and forth between 4/4 and 3/4. Count this one out "1–2–3–4/1–2–3/1–2–3–4/1–2–3" with each numeral given an equal quarter note duration. Don't lose beat 1!

## "Dyers Eve" Intro Riff from ...And Justice for All

♩=102
**Half-time feel**

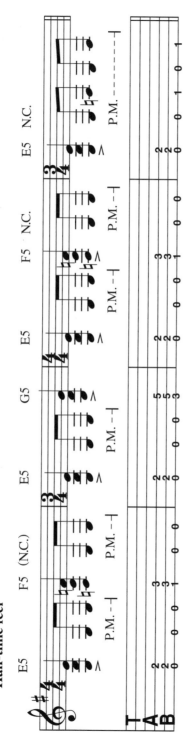

Let's push the trickiness quotient up a notch now. In the following riff from "Leper Messiah," the time shifts from 4/4 to 5/4 to 4/4 to 3/4! Once again, each beat is of equal length, but the measures aren't. Take your time getting to know the rhythmic feel of this line before taking it to your guitar. If you can't sing or tap the rhythms out correctly, the addition of your instrument won't help much. This isn't the easiest phrase in the world, so take your time here.

## "Leper Messiah" Post-Chorus Riff from Master of Puppets

♩=136

## "Master of Puppets" Verse Riff from *Master of Puppets*

In the following riff from "Master of Puppets," a new wrinkle appears. In the final measure, the time shifts from 4/4 to 5/8, so the basic pulse changes from a quarter note beat to an eighth note beat. Try counting the phrase out by including eighth notes in the 4/4 measures, verbalizing those notes with "and." In other words, a measure of 4/4 plus a measure of 5/8 would be counted as "1–and–2–and–3–and–4–and–1–2–3–4–5." All of the "ands" and numerals above should be of equal duration.

Confused? Try counting it all out while listening to the recording that came with this book to get a better idea of how such a transition should sound.

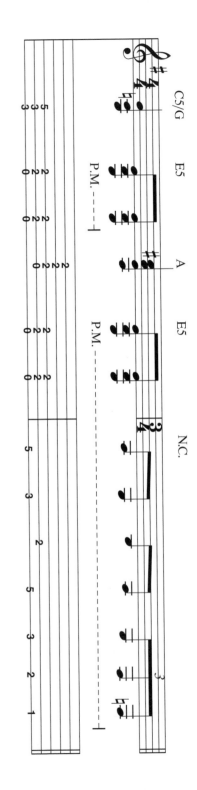

TRACK 25

♩ = 220

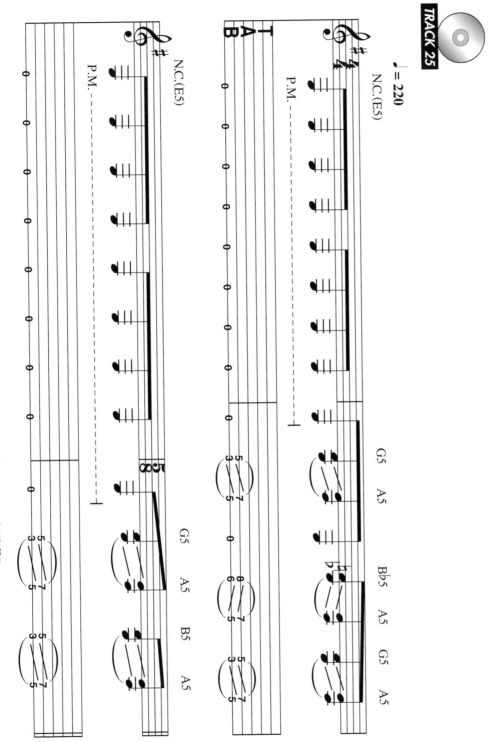

In the chorus riff from "Hit the Lights," the measures alternate between 4/4 and 7/8 time. The count for this one should be "1–and–2–and–3–and–4–and–1–2–3–4–5–6–7."

Starting to make sense? If you like, you can think of the measure of 7/8 as if it were a measure of 4/4 with its last eighth note lopped off. Some musicians like to approach it like this, while others find it only adds to the confusion! Whatever process helps your comprehension can and should be employed. However, try to avoid simply "feeling" the shift or thinking of the vocal in this particular example in lieu of actually counting things out and understanding what's really going on.

# "Hit the Lights" Chorus Riff from *Kill 'Em All*

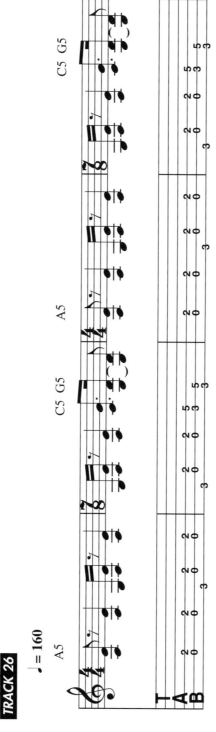

The following example from "Battery" includes the same 4/4 to 7/8 shift, but this time most of the example is taken up by rests—you can really concentrate on your counting with this one. Try looping this around on itself until you've got it down solid. If you try to simply "feel" your way through these transitions, you won't be able to build the skills and confidence needed to navigate your way through full songs. The band's writing is often jam-packed with these shifts—and we're only skimming the surface here in terms of difficulty!

# "Battery" Break from *Master of Puppets*

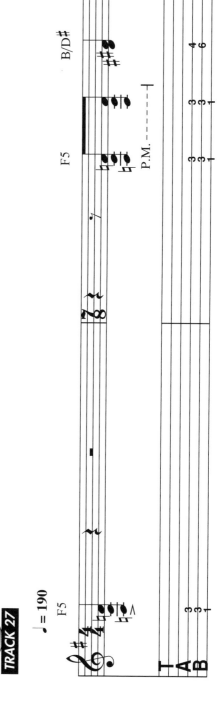

# "Disposable Heroes" Chorus Excerpt from *Master of Puppets*

Here's an interesting riff from "Disposable Heroes" that includes three measures of 4/4, one of 7/8, and one of 2/4. The first three measures are a good test of your knowledge of ties, dotted notes and 16th notes—watch out for those 16ths in the 7/8 measure!

TRACK 28

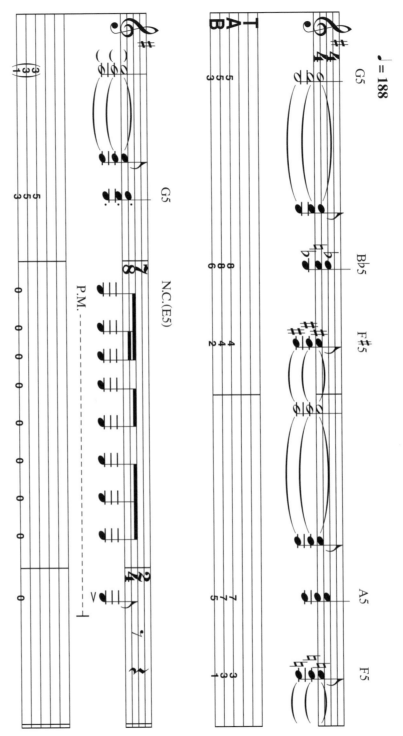

Words and Music by James Hetfield, Lars Ulrich and Kirk Hammett
Copyright © 1986 Creeping Death Music (ASCAP)
International Copyright Secured   All Rights Reserved

Musicians often speak somewhat mysteriously about *metric modulation*, and it's a phenomenon that can be difficult to understand at times. The previous examples, in which the quarter note and eighth note alternate as the basic pulse, are a case in point. The following excerpt from "Eye of the Beholder" includes a different sort of metric modulation. As the time signature shifts from 4/4 to 12/8, so does the basic pulse, so that a quarter note in the original time signature becomes a dotted quarter note in the new one. Put another way, three eighth notes (which add up to a dotted quarter note) take the same amount of musical time as a quarter note in 4/4. 12/8 is often thought of not so much as a time signature but as a "feel"—one in which an eighth note triplet exists in the space of each quarter note in 4/4 time. It's often found in slow blues settings: over the basic 4/4 beat, a drummer may play a steady triplet pattern on his or her ride cymbal while the bassist may also play the same rhythm. In the next example, beats 3 and 4 in the second measure feature "broken" eighth note triplets that prepare us for the transition to 12/8. In fact, the final two notes in measure 2 give us the new pulse—they go by at the same speed that each of the 12 eighth notes in measures 3 and 4 will.

Before you tackle playing this one, try the following exercise: tap your foot in 4/4 at a slow tempo and say aloud "one-trip-let, two-trip-let, three-trip-let, four-trip-let" with each syllable of equal duration. Careful listening to the record-ing (while counting along) should clear up any confusion that remains.

## "Eye of the Beholder" Excerpt from ...*And Justice for All*

**TRACK 29**

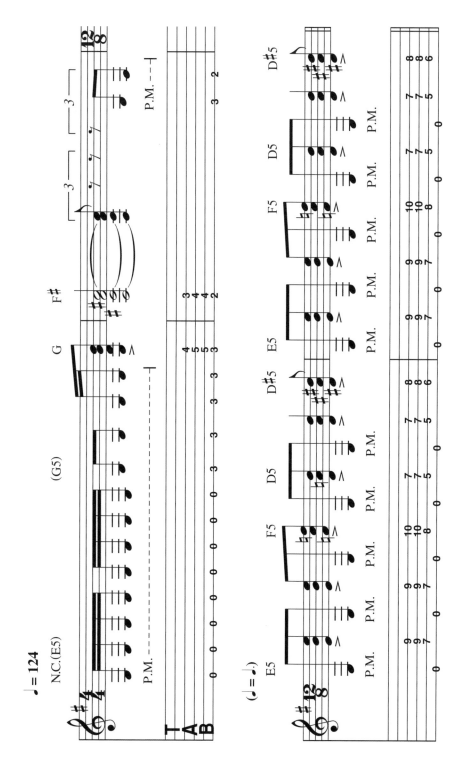

Words and Music by James Hetfield, Lars Ulrich and Kirk Hammett
Copyright © 1988 Creeping Death Music (ASCAP)
International Copyright Secured   All Rights Reserved

Finally, let's take a look at the introduction to "Blackened." This one is tough because it's fast, difficult to play, and changes time signature several times. There's no metric modulation to worry about, but that's small consolation. You're going to want to really take your time here, slowing things down, counting them out, and using the accom-panying CD as a reference to check that you're playing things correctly.

It's an exhausting, whirlwind chunk of Metallica's unique songwriting style at its most ornate, and it will most likely take some time to get together. Don't get discouraged or be impatient. Kirk Hammett and James Hetfield didn't just roll out of bed one day and nail playing like this over their morning coffee, so don't be too hard on yourself if you're not playing it perfectly before breakfast is over!

# "Blackened" Intro Riff from ...And Justice for All

♩ = 182

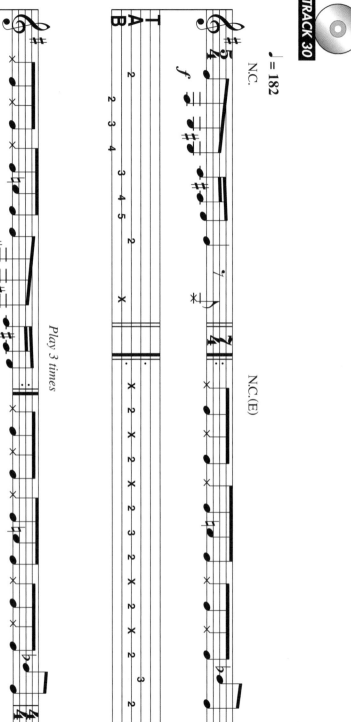

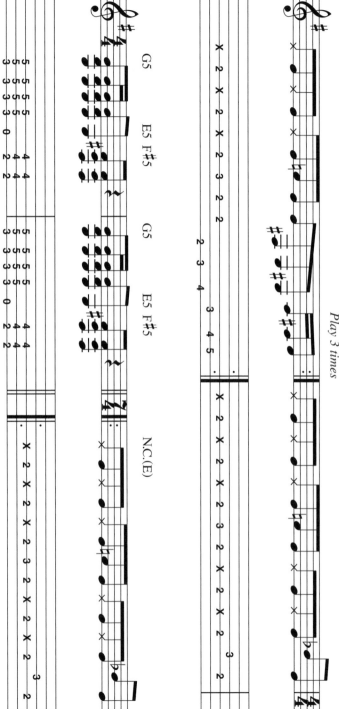

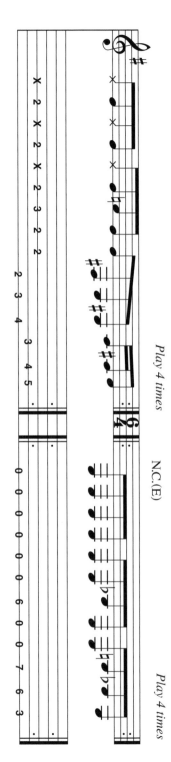

# CHAPTER 6

## Articulation Techniques

It's time to shift gears again and zero in on some of the various articulation techniques you'll encounter in Metallica's music (and in guitar music in general). You may already be familiar with these techniques, but a little refresher never hurts, and you'll get to learn some more killer riffs and licks.

*Articulation* in music refers to the various ways a given note can be expressed, those little details that give pitches and rhythms life and emotion and shape. Articulation techniques such as vibrato, *glissando* (sliding into or away from notes), *legato* (playing smoothly from note to note), and *staccato* (playing notes short and clipped) keep things interesting and are absolutely crucial in Metallica's music. They transform power chords and single-note lines into the menacing, mosh-inducing epics we hear on the albums—they are not to be omitted when recreating these songs ourselves.

Before tackling the examples, let's look at a few articulation techniques.

### Palm Muting

We've already seen this quite a bit. You partially mute a string by anchoring your picking hand on the bridge right at the point at which the strings reach the saddles. Don't move your hand too far forward or you'll totally obscure the actual pitches being played. Palm mutes are one way the band gets a staccato sound and lots of distorted "crunch."

### Vibrato

The fretting hand rapidly bends and releases the given string enough to create this vocal effect, but not enough to significantly change the pitch of the note. Vibrato can be slight, moderate, or wide and very exaggerated. It's often used on sustained pitches as they begin to die away. Try stabilizing your fretting hand a bit as you "vibrate" a note by letting the neck sit firmly in the nook between your thumb and index finger and wiggling your fretting finger(s) slightly on the string.

### Slides

Often called a *glissando* in the conservatory, a slide can aid in creating a legato (smooth) effect and can be a nice way to get from one place to another on the fingerboard. Slides can also be quite vocal or horn-like if used skillfully and can create the sense of notes "running together" without discrete separation. Merely slide your finger(s) up or down as indicated from one pitch to the next while keeping pressure on the string. Guitarists frequently slide from (or to) "nowhere"—that is, a slide begins or ends a few frets away from a target note so that we hear the approach (or departure) but not necessarily from or to a specific pitch. This is in contrast to slides that are indicated to clearly connect one note to another.

### Hammer-Ons

Instead of picking every note, you pick a first note and then hammer on from one fretting hand finger to the next to sound the pitch. Mostly, this involves bringing down the finger with enough force to produce the note without a new strike of the pick, and it's easier to accomplish on a guitar with low action (a distortion-saturated tone doesn't hurt either). Hammer-ons (and pull-offs, for that matter) are a great way to add a legato feeling to your playing. Alternate picking every single note you play can make you sound a little too mechanical.

The opposing approach to hammer-ons, pull-offs are executed by simultaneously lifting a finger and pulling down slightly on the string to sound a lower pitch. It's that little pull down that really gets the new note to ring out and, once again, it's easier to accomplish on a low-action guitar.

## Trills

This is a very rapid fluctuation between two pitches. Basically, you move back and forth between two notes as fast as you can. For instance, if you see a half note with a trill marking above it and a note in parenthesis following it, pick the first note once and hammer-on and pull-between the two notes as many times as you can within the allotted two beats. On the guitar, trills are only possible between two notes on the same string (obviously!).

Let's look at some of these techniques in action.

Here's a four-measure stretch of slides from "Holier than Thou." Each of these slides—two-note barre shapes on the high E and B strings—should be played with the index finger. Begin the descent on beat 2 of each measure, and move down a few frets before resting on beat 3. These are some of the "slides to nowhere" mentioned earlier.

## "Holier than Thou" Solo Excerpt from *Metallica*

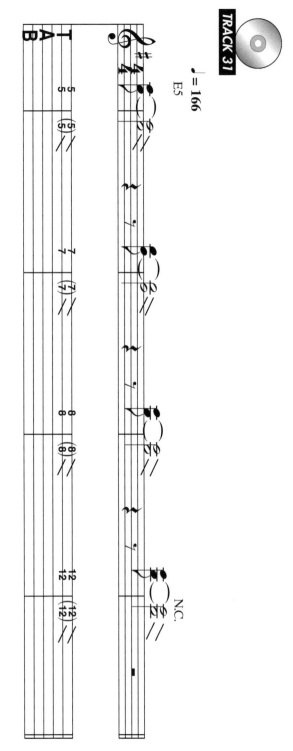

TRACK 31

Here's a simple figure from "My Friend of Misery" that employs carefully placed palm-muting and some vibrato at the end. Notice the tiny "G" that immediately precedes the final "A" in the example. This is a *grace note*, a common adornment that takes up no measurable musical time. On the second beat of this measure, use your ring finger on the D string's 5th fret, strike the note, and immediately slide up two frets to the A without picking again. Apply vibrato while the note sustains.

## "My Friend of Misery" Intro Figure from *Metallica*

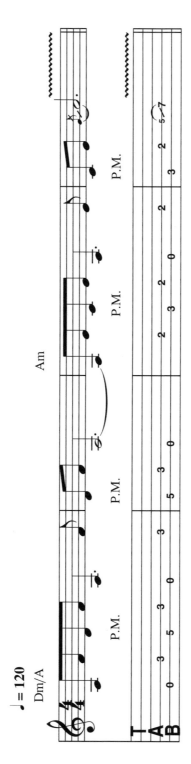

Words and Music by James Hetfield, Lars Ulrich and Jason Newsted
Copyright © 1991 Creeping Death Music (ASCAP)
International Copyright Secured   All Rights Reserved

The following excerpt from "Sad but True" includes slides, vibrato, and palm muting. Play the entire example first with none of the indicated articulations, and then go back and apply them in the proper places and see what a difference it makes—the music comes to life! Try beginning each D-string slide with your pinky, about two frets below the "target" tone of A (7th fret), and add vibrato in the appropriate places by really shaking your index finger. Tune your strings down a whole step for this song.

# "Sad but True" Interlude Lick from Metallica

**TRACK 33**

Tune down 1 whole step:
(low to high) D-G-C-F-A-D

♩ = 86

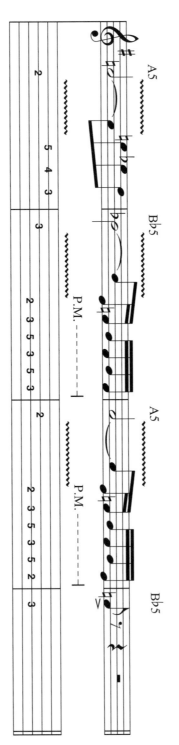

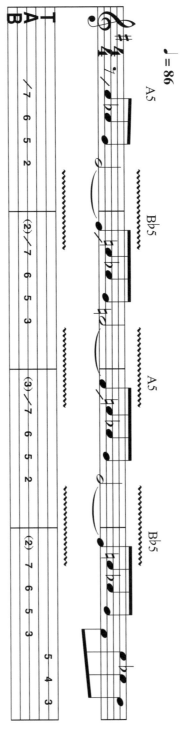

Next, let's look at a riff from "Wherever I May Roam" that includes trills, hammer-ons, and slides. After the first beat, use your index finger on the A string's 7th fret throughout the example, putting you in position to trill to your middle finger at the end of measures 1 and 3; for most people, these are the best digits for trilling. In measure 2, play the G on the D string's 5th fret with your index finger, slide up two frets to sound the A without re-picking, and then finish by hitting the F on the A string with your middle finger.

## "Wherever I May Roam" Intro Riff from *Metallica*

 **TRACK 34**

**Half-time feel**

♩ = 128

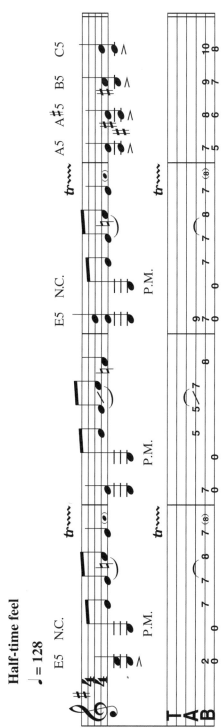

Here's a simple riff from "The Struggle Within." Play the power chords in this one with two consecutive downstrokes and palm-mute the first. Both slides should be executed with the ring finger as dictated by general positioning, while the G-string hammer-ons should be played with your middle and ring fingers.

## "The Struggle Within" Half-Time Interlude Riff from *Metallica*

 **TRACK 35**

**Half-time feel**

♩ = 180

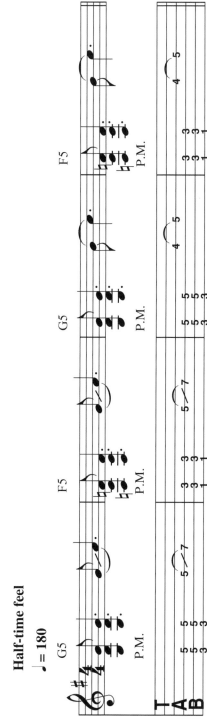

Next, check out this wicked riff from the lycanthrope-inspired thrasher "Of Wolf and Man." The tempo is slow enough to allow all downstrokes in the first measure, except for the muted 16th notes, which should be alternate-picked. In the second measure, pick the D on the A string (beat 2) once, then hammer on to your ring finger, pull off to your index finger, and then pull off to the open string—four notes on one pickstroke! You may want to isolate this 16th phrase and repeat it many times out of the context of the riff itself—it's a great little exercise for hammer-on and pull-off strength.

## "Of Wolf and Man" Verse Riff from Metallica

TRACK 36

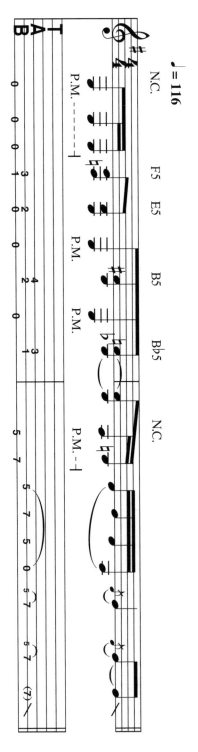

Words and Music by James Hetfield, Lars Ulrich and Kirk Hammett
Copyright © 1991 Creeping Death Music (ASCAP)
International Copyright Secured   All Rights Reserved

Let's return to "Sad but True" for a killer riff with pull-offs that practically defines the phrase "head-banging." Don't forget to tune down a whole step here for that extra-heavy effect. After the bone-crushing E5 power chords that begin the phrase, use your pinky to pull-off from the 5th fret to the open A string, your index finger for the 1st-fret pull-off, and your middle finger for the low E-string pull-off. This is challenging because the pinky is the weakest finger by far and may not want to cooperate in pulling-off and adding vibrato to the final note of the phrase. Also, it's a bit of a stretch down to the index finger at the 1st fret. Then again, no one ever said that playing great guitar was easy—and if they did, well, they lied!

## "Sad but True" Intro Riff from *Metallica*

TRACK 37

Tune down 1 step:
(low to high) D-G-C-F-A-D
♩ = 86

Words and Music by James Hetfield and Lars Ulrich
Copyright © 1991 Creeping Death Music (ASCAP)
International Copyright Secured   All Rights Reserved

The section on the next page from "My Friend of Misery" is harmonized in 3rds above by another guitar, and it's a real stretch and pull-off workout. I hope your pinky strength has improved since the previous example, because you're gonna need it here! Basically, your pinky pulls off to your index finger from the 10th to the 5th fret repeatedly in measures 1, 2, 5, and 6, while your middle finger grabs the Fs at the 6th fret of the B string. Things get a bit easier in measures 3 and 4, as the pull-off from the 8th fret to the 5th is a lot less demanding; your index finger should be barring the top two strings at the 5th fret here. At the end of measure 6, slide your pinky up the high E string all the way to the 17th fret for more five-fret pull-offs (things are a little closer in this region of the neck, thankfully). The final measure of the phrase is all pinky!

# "My Friend of Misery" Interlude Lick from *Metallica*

TRACK 38

♩ = 120

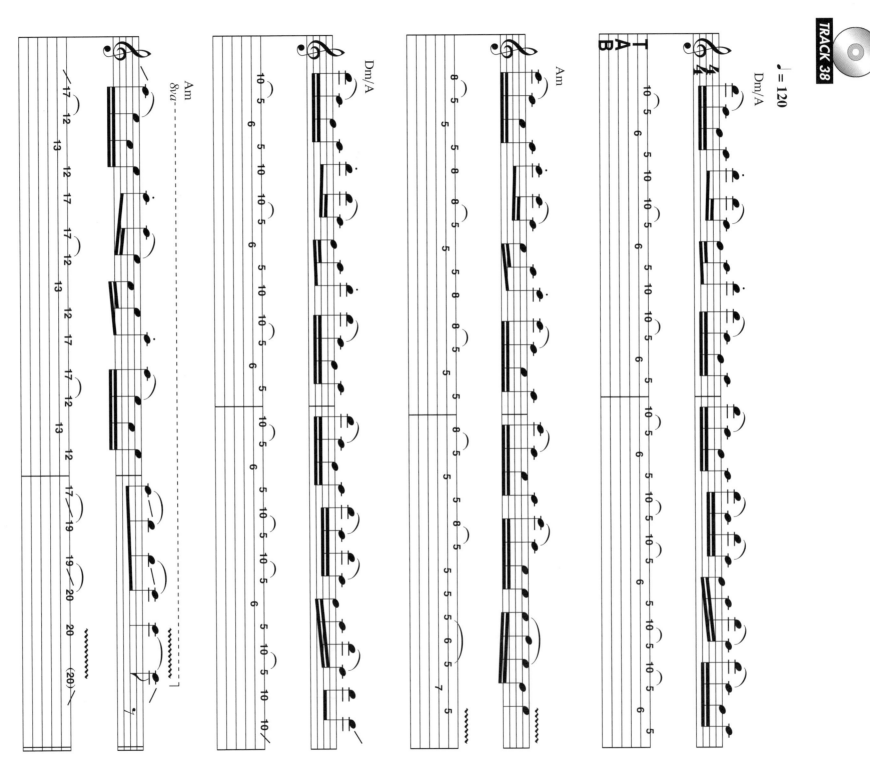

Words and Music by James Hetfield, Lars Ulrich and Jason Newsted
Copyright © 1991 Creeping Death Music (ASCAP)
International Copyright Secured   All Rights Reserved

# CHAPTER 7

## Double Stops

*Double stops*, or *dyads* as they're often called by the more formal-minded among us, are simply two notes played simultaneously. We've seen a lot of these already, as the traditional two-note power chord is obviously a double stop, but in this section we're going to examine the way they can be applied in solos, usually on the higher strings of the guitar. Kirk Hammett creates the majority of his solos with notes taken from a few choice scales—minor pentatonic (in E, E–G–A–B–D), Dorian mode (in E, E–F♯–G–A–B–C♯–D), and Aeolian mode (again, in E, E–F♯–G–A–B–C–D). But he also frequently peppers his single-note lines with double stops that add lots of hard-edged blues feeling. Let's take a look at some of his licks.

Our first excerpt is from his solo on "Through the Never" and is played over a B minor backdrop. The notes here are squarely in the B minor pentatonic scale (B–D–E–F♯–A). Begin the lick with your ring finger and stay strictly in 7th position (your index finger should play all of notes on the 7th fret, your middle finger takes all notes on the 8th, etc.). The double stops in the phrase, D and F♯ (a major 3rd apart) should be played with your index finger barring the G and B strings.

## "Through the Never" Solo Excerpt from *Metallica*

TRACK 39

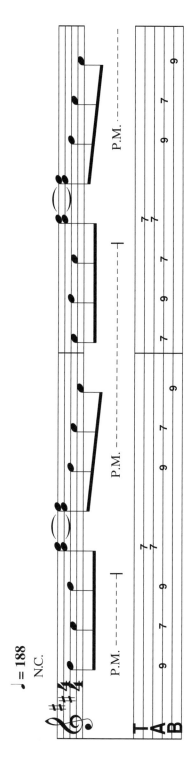

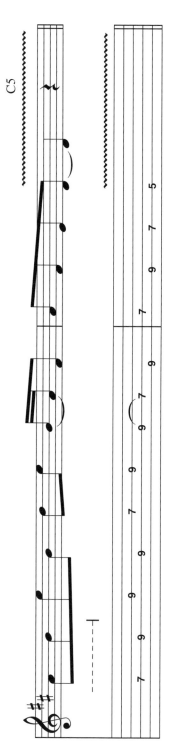

Words and Music by James Hetfield, Lars Ulrich and Kirk Hammett
Copyright © 1991 Creeping Death Music (ASCAP)
International Copyright Secured   All Rights Reserved

Double stops come in many forms. Hammett plays mostly two-note groupings a 3rd or 4th interval apart, but octaves do pop up as well. Sixths are quite popular with blues and country guitarists.

The example below from "Don't Tread on Me" includes double stops in 12th position over an E5 riff with the ring and index fingers barring the 14th and 12th frets, respectively.

## "Don't Tread on Me" Solo Excerpt from Metallica

TRACK 40

Tune down 1/2 step:
(low to high) Eb-Ab-Db-Gb-Bb-Eb

♩. = 104

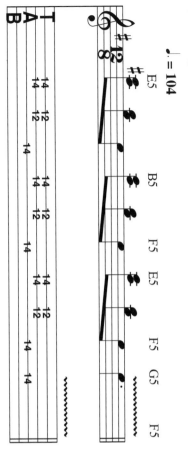

## "Don't Tread on Me" Solo Excerpt from Metallica

TRACK 41

Tune down 1/2 step:
(low to high) Eb-Ab-Db-Gb-Bb-Eb

♩. = 104

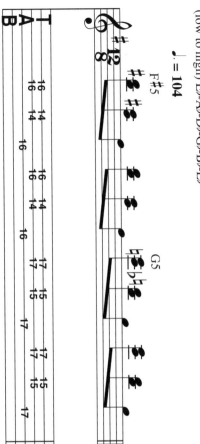

Here's another nifty double stop lick from the same song. It's a return to the figure above, this time moving up chromatically to follow the ascending F#5 and G5 chords. Don't worry about staying in position for this one; when the figure moves up, merely slide your hand up a fret to get to the lick played over G5.

Here's the very cool opening phrase from the "Sad but True" solo, which begins with a minor 3rd interval shape sliding up the G and B strings (use your middle and index fingers, respectively). The G♯ and B against the E5 chord lend things a temporary major flavor, unusual for the band, but Hammett quickly reverts to E minor pentatonic licks in the 12th fret "box" and throws in a number of barred, index-finger double stops to boot.

## "Sad but True" Solo Excerpt from Metallica

**TRACK 42**

Tune down 1 step:
(low to high) D-G-C-F-A-D

♩ = 86

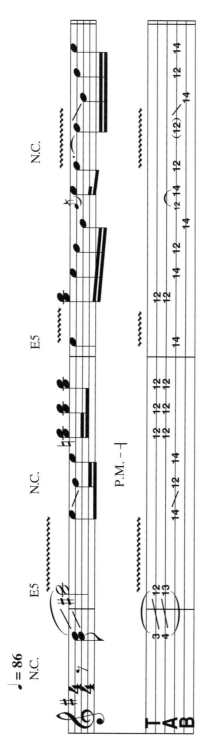

This two-measure phrase from the "Of Wolf and Man" solo finds Hammett once again putting a major touch to the music with a B♭–D double stop played over a B♭5 power chord. He's in 15th position here, using his index finger to barre the G and B strings at the 15th fret, while the ring finger is employed for the 17th fret barres. The rhythmic aspect of the phrase, with its 16th note funk flavor, is one of its coolest attributes.

## "Of Wolf and Man" Solo Excerpt from Metallica

**TRACK 43**

♩ = 116

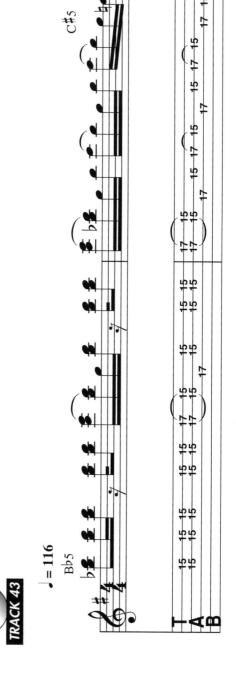

In the following excerpt from "Cure," we get more 16th note funkiness and barred double stops. Note that the one-finger barres played on the D and G strings include two notes a 4th apart (A and D, B and E), while the same shape on the G and B strings creates a major 3rd (the D and F♯ double stop that ends measure 2). To play the final measure, slide your middle finger up the B string from the 8th to the 10th frets, and then use your index and middle fingers for the sliding double stops on beat 2. Your index finger will now be in position to perform the slide up the G string from the 11th to the 14th fret on beat 3.

# "Cure" Solo Excerpt from *Load*

**TRACK 44**

Tune down 1/2 step:
(low to high) E♭-A♭-D♭-G♭-B♭-E♭

♩ = 120

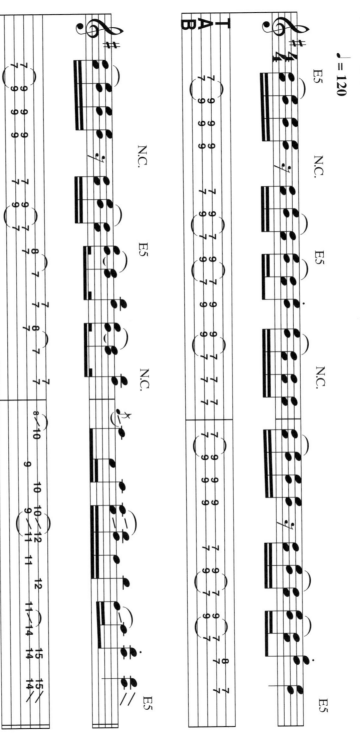

Words and Music by James Hetfield and Lars Ulrich
Copyright © 1996 Creeping Death Music (ASCAP)
International Copyright Secured   All Rights Reserved

Finally, here's a double stop phrase in octaves taken from Hammett's "Ride the Lightning" solo. These are a bit tricky in that they're not on consecutive strings; they require you to slightly flatten your index finger (on the D string) to mute the open G, while your pinky takes care of business on the B string above. You may also have a hard time moving both fingers in parallel fashion, so take it slow and work the line back up to speed over time. Jazz guitar genius Wes Montgomery was famous for his lightning-fast octave playing, but Hammett has taken a page from his book and incorporated the technique into his own solo style, adding a new wrinkle to his ever-evolving approach. See if you can make octaves work for you, starting now with the following lick.

# "Ride the Lightning" Solo Excerpt from *Ride the Lightning*

**TRACK 45**

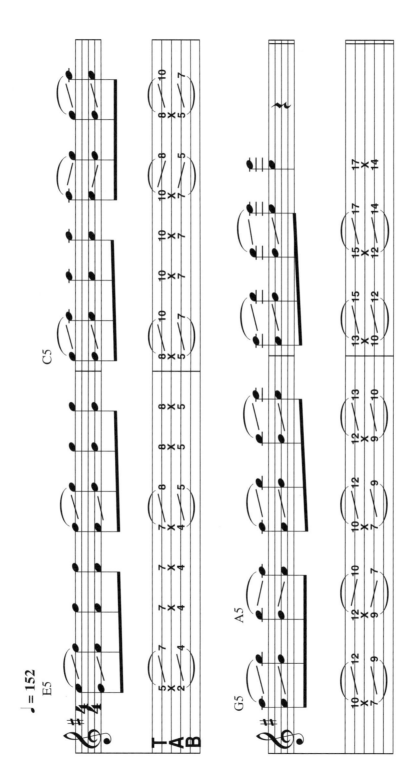

Words and Music by James Hetfield, Lars Ulrich, Cliff Burton and Dave Mustaine
Copyright © 1984 Creeping Death Music (ASCAP)
International Copyright Secured   All Rights Reserved

# CHAPTER 8

## String Bending

The first book in this series touched briefly upon string bending but now we're going to really examine the different ways in which this essential technique can be employed, as well as the many forms of bends you'll encounter both in the music of Metallica and elsewhere. Among the myriad string-bending possibilities are variations in distance (half steps, whole steps, and more), number of strings bent at once, direction of pull (towards the floor or away), and the amount of time a bend is held.

Let's jump right in, with an excerpt from the solo on "My Friend of Misery." The phrase is taken from the F♯ minor pentatonic scale (F♯–A–B–C♯–E) and is played in 2nd position. The bends below should be played with your ring finger, although the use of the pinky would also be correct—and, in some ways, preferable. It's just that the pinky isn't very strong and the ring finger should have no problem with the stretch involved here.

In the example below, the B string is bent up a whole step to match the F♯ on the high E string that immediately follows it; this gives you the opportunity to hear whether or not you're bending in tune. Bending skill takes time and work to develop; hand strength must be acquired, as well as the intuitive sense of how far to push the string (which, of course, varies from guitar to guitar). Begin the lick by pushing the B string towards your head with the ring finger, with the middle finger on the string just behind it to aid in the task. The two bends at the end of the measure are a bit easier, but be careful not to push past your target note (F♯) when you add that 3rd finger to the B string—you're working with less resistance now.

TRACK 46

## "My Friend of Misery" Solo Excerpt from *Metallica*

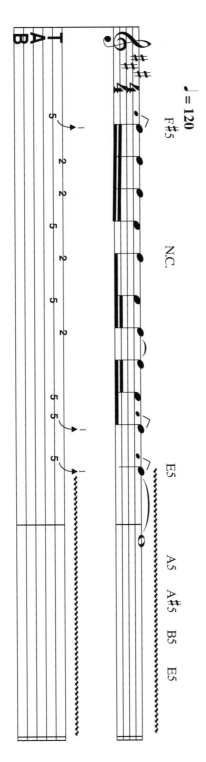

Adding vibrato to a bend, as in the lick we've just played, is a common practice and one that lends things a vocal quality while helping to maintain pitch over a long note duration. Many guitarists wait just a moment before beginning to vibrate a bent note. Also, you may notice as you work your way through this chapter that the vast majority of bending is done with the ring finger and the pinky, which allows for the index and middle fingers to be added in behind to aid in the pushing and pulling of the string.

In this next example, all bends should be played with the ring finger. The lick begins in 7th position and climbs to 12th halfway through by means of a ring-finger slide up the G string to the 14th fret. One excellent way of checking your pitch accuracy is by first playing the pitch that you're bending to, and then actually bending the string to see if you're in tune. For instance, play only the F# on the B string's 7th fret, and then execute the bend in measure 1 to see if you're on the mark or if adjustments need to be made. Also, notice in the second measure that the bend is held a moment before being released to its unbent state (and then pulled off to the index finger at the 7th fret). This is called a *bend-and-release* and it's a common technique that Kirk Hammett puts to good use.

# "Seek & Destroy" Solo Excerpt from *Kill 'Em All*

Words and Music by James Hetfield and Lars Ulrich
Copyright © 1983 Creeping Death Music (ASCAP)
International Copyright Secured   All Rights Reserved

**TRACK 48**

## "Fixxxer" Post-Solo Interlude Excerpt from *ReLoad*

Here's a riff from "Fixxxer" that's a little bit different. First, all of the bends are on the D string; this is lower than you'll find most string-bending takes place, and it requires you to pull towards your feet rather than push towards your head. Also, there are three different bending distances here: quarter step, half step, and whole step. The quarter step bends here should be played with the index finger, which is also somewhat unusual. Your target is squarely between the notes G and G♯, which may take a little adjustment. The real challenge, however, comes in the second measure. Pull the D string up a whole step for the first bend, then execute a half step *pre-bend and release*. This technique involves bending the string the specified distance before striking the note, so you have to know both what the target pitch should sound like and how far the string should be bent without hearing it first. Try this: Play the four eighth notes that begin the measure, and then play B, B♭, and A on the D string (on the 9th, 8th, and 7th frets, respectively). Those are the target pitches you should match when you go back and add the bends as written. Don't worry if pre-bending gives you fits at first—it's an advanced technique and requires a lot of practice before it becomes second nature.

Tune down 1/2 step:
(low to high) E♭-A♭-D♭-G♭-B♭-E♭

♩ = 108

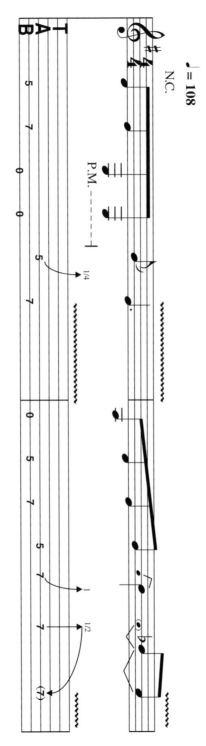

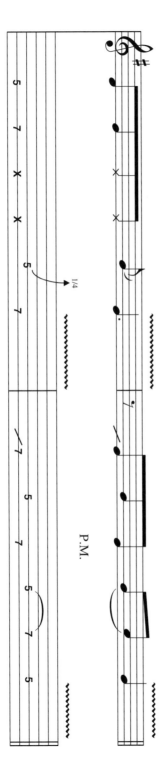

This next example, from "Through the Never," includes repeated half step bends on the A string which should be played with your ring finger pulling toward the floor. There's a new wrinkle in measure 2, though—a whole step bend from E to F♯ that is pushed even further as it sustains. This step-and-a-half bend, all the way up to G, is known as an *overbend*, and it's another tricky technique that requires you to know what that G sounds like without fretting it first. As with the previous example, go ahead and play the G at the 10th fret of the A string first so you know what you're shooting for, and then go back and play the lick as written and see if you can get it tune. Overbending, particularly on the A string, takes a fair amount of strength that can only be acquired through steady practice and repetition. A very cool effect is created in measure 3 by gradually releasing the bend back down to its unbent position; give a listen to the recording if you're not sure how this should sound.

# "Through the Never" Solo Excerpt from *Metallica*

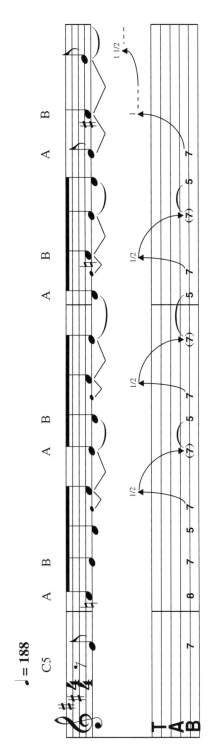

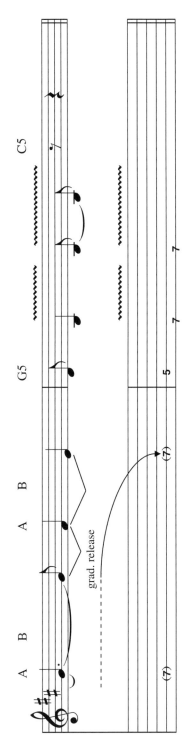

Words and Music by James Hetfield, Lars Ulrich and Kirk Hammett
Copyright © 1991 Creeping Death Music (ASCAP)
International Copyright Secured   All Rights Reserved

In the following excerpt from "My Friend of Misery," strike the open high E string and bend the B string up to match it at the same time, creating a nice effect that brings to mind both Jimmy Page and the sound of pedal steel guitar. You'll want to stay in 1st position here so that your middle finger plays all of the notes on the 2nd fret and your ring finger takes all of those on the 3rd (including the bend). The fact that the open high E string is ringing while you bend the B should leave little doubt as to whether you're in tune here or not!

# "My Friend of Misery" Interlude Excerpt from *Metallica*

TRACK 50

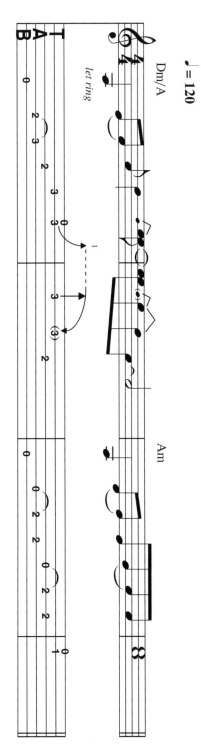

Next up is a lick from Hammett's "Fixxxer" solo in which the ring finger is used to bend the B string up a whole step and hold it; the high E string is then added to the mix. This is often referred to as a *unison bend*, and it requires great accuracy because both notes involved are the same pitch. If the bend is even slightly off, you'll hear it. The fact that the bend is held for so long (over two full measures) will put a lot of strain on your fretting hand—if your strength starts to go and the bend slips, the intonation will go out the window. If you're having this problem, or if you're new to string bending in general, make it a part of your daily practice routine, but don't overdo it. The last thing you want to do is give yourself tendonitis, so temper your enthusiasm a bit and limit your bending work to, say, 15 or 20 minutes a day at first. The final measure of this lick is tough as well, requiring you to use your ring finger for everything; bend at the 17th fret, slide up to the 19th fret and bend there, and then finish with some tasty vibrato before playing that open A string.

## "Fixxxer" Solo Excerpt from *ReLoad*

TRACK 51

Tune down 1/2 step:
(low to high) Eb–Ab–Db–Gb–Bb–Eb

Words and Music by James Hetfield, Lars Ulrich and Kirk Hammett
Copyright © 1997 Creeping Death Music (ASCAP)
International Copyright Secured   All Rights Reserved

Three distinct bending techniques are used in the following excerpt from "Through the Never." In the first three measures, bend the G string with your ring finger, and then follow with the double stop by barring the top two strings with your index finger. In measure 4, execute a pre-bend and release, pushing the G string up a whole step from B to C# before striking it and releasing the bend on beat 2 (watch that intonation!). In the final two measures, execute the unison bends with your index finger on the B string and your ring finger pushing up the G string a whole step to match it.

# "Through the Never" Solo Excerpt from *Metallica*

TRACK 52

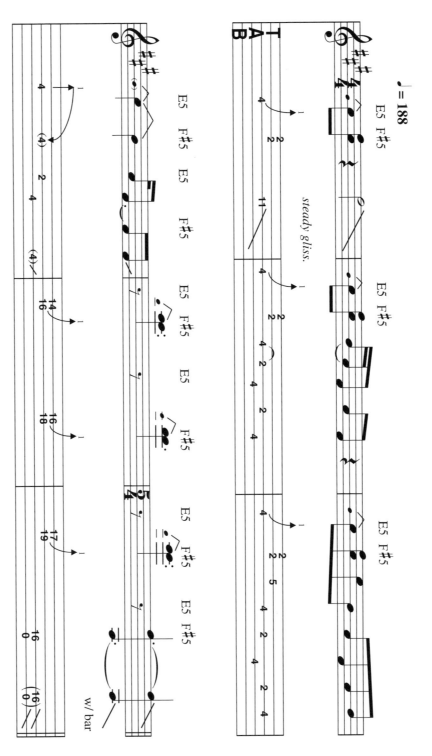

Words and Music by James Hetfield, Lars Ulrich and Kirk Hammett
Copyright © 1991 Creeping Death Music (ASCAP)
International Copyright Secured   All Rights Reserved

In the lick below from "The Struggle Within," push the B string up a whole step with the ring finger, and then alter-nate that note with the same pitch on the high E string's 12th fret. It's another endurance test, as that B-string bend lasts a long time and cannot be allowed to slip at all. Because the pitch of the bend matches that of the unbent string, any wavering will be immediately apparent.

# "The Struggle Within" Solo Excerpt from *Metallica*

**TRACK 53**

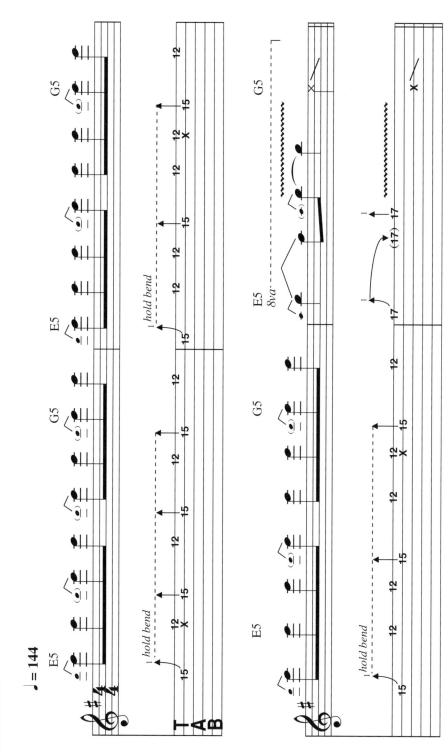

Here's an unusual lick from "Cure," in which both the B and high E strings are bent simultaneously with the same finger! It's not as hard as it sounds. The first 17th-fret bend is up a half step, quickly followed by a whole step bend. By this time you should be coming up against the B string anyway, so on the third bend merely allow it to slip under your ring finger and push both up at the same time. Bend them up a half step twice, and then up a whole step twice and release at the end of the second measure. The heavier the gauge of your strings, the harder it will be to pull this off—.010's are ideal for this style, as anything lighter tends to lack depth and thickness. Heavy-gauge strings sound great and cut through a band with more punch, but their sheer thickness makes pulling off bends like this much tougher.

# "Cure" Solo Excerpt from *Load*

Tune down 1/2 step:
(low to high) E♭-A♭-D♭-G♭-B♭-E♭

♩ = 120

N.C.
*8va*

B♭5/F

N.C.
(*8va*)

*Both strings caught and
bent w/L.H. ring finger.

Finally, let's look at phrase from the "Don't Tread on Me" solo involving double stop bends in which each string is pushed up a different distance with the same finger. Sound impossible? It's not. In fact, because the G string is thicker than the B string (the two strings employed here), it's really not that hard at all. Just barre the strings with your ring finger and push, using the B string as your guide. If you're applying equal pressure to both strings, when you bend the C# to D, the A on the G string below should reach B almost of its own accord. A little practice with this move should yield results fairly quickly.

# "Don't Tread on Me" Solo Excerpt from *Metallica*

TRACK 55

Tune down 1/2 step:
(low to high) Eb-Ab-Db-Gb-Bb-Eb

♩. = 104

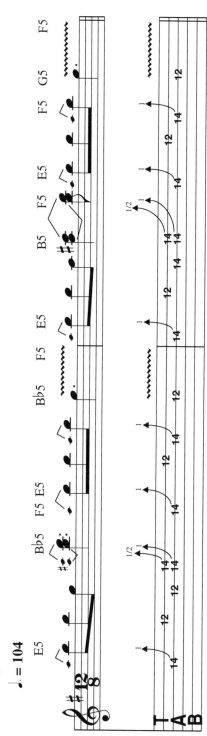

Words and Music by James Hetfield and Lars Ulrich
Copyright © 1991 Creeping Death Music (ASCAP)
International Copyright Secured   All Rights Reserved

Remember that Rome wasn't built in a day. Top notch bending chops won't be either!

# CHAPTER 9

## Specialized Techniques

There are a number of specialized techniques that can prove to be valuable additions to your playing. The following is by no means exhaustive but may open your eyes a bit to these unusual and often very intriguing methods.

### Natural Harmonics

These bell-like tones are produced by lightly placing your finger on a given string, right above the fret wire, but not pushing down to the wood to sound the note as usual. To play the following example from "Nothing Else Matters," place your index finger on the top three strings above the metal just past the 12th fret. Again, your finger should be being barely touching the strings and not exerting any pressure at all. Strike the low E string, and then play the indicated harmonics and open strings, letting everything ring for their full durations. Loop the measure a few times until you're producing crystalline, shimmering harmonics.

## "Nothing Else Matters" Intro from *Metallica*

Words and Music by James Hetfield and Lars Ulrich
Copyright © 1991 Creeping Death Music (ASCAP)
International Copyright Secured   All Rights Reserved

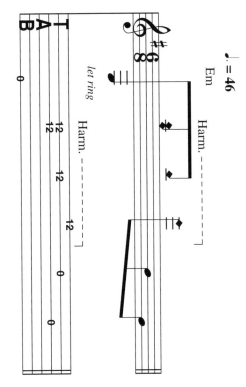

♪. = 46

Em

let ring

Harm.

Harm.

Harm.

### Volume Swells

Intriguing effects can be created by the manipulation of your guitar's volume. The basic approach is to pick as usual, but also curl your pinky around the volume knob and turn it with this digit, rather than twisting it between your thumb and forefinger. Obviously, this requires a guitar with a volume knob close enough to the strings to facilitate such a maneuver (a Stratocaster or Strat-style guitar is ideal). A volume swell usually starts with the knob rolled off completely, so that a given pitch is struck in silence and then appears to come from out of nowhere as the volume is raised while the note sustains. Let's look at a few examples.

Here's an excerpt from "Master of Puppets" that's played entirely on the D string. Your fretting hand has the easier task here, with a sequence of ascending notes made up of whole and half note rhythms. Begin with your volume off, and then strike the E that opens the phrase while simultaneously rolling the knob in a clockwise direction. The challenge here is not only in the physical execution, but also in both raising the volume gradually to give it that swelling effect and quickly rolling it off again to begin the next swell in silence. It's a technique that may take some time to master, but it can become a beautiful, artistic part of your playing once it's under your control.

## "Master of Puppets" Interlude from *Master of Puppets*

TRACK 57

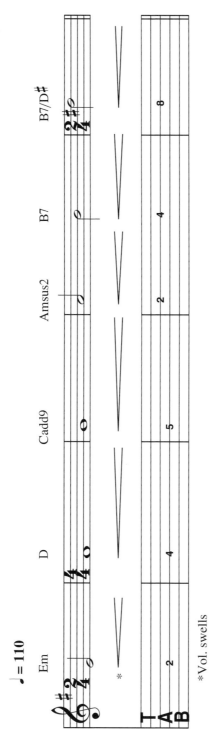

*Vol. swells

Let's go back to "Nothing Else Matters." Strike the harmonics (in silence) by placing your finger lightly across the top three strings above the 12th fret, and then roll the volume up gradually. If you have a vibrato ("whammy") bar, depress it slowly to lower them each by a half step. If your guitar has a fixed bridge and/or tailpiece, merely let the notes decay as the volume swells.

## "Nothing Else Matters" Intro from *Metallica*

TRACK 58

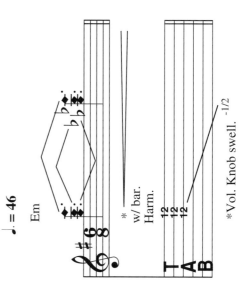

*Vol. Knob swell.

The following excerpt from "My Friend of Misery" is a bit more involved, in that it's longer, has quicker rhythms, and includes a few bends that sound particularly cool when swelled up from out of silence. The picking hand approach is the same as we've seen in the previous two examples, only this time you have to be faster on your toes to get the volume knob back down to zero, as the notes are coming at a quicker pace than before. The whole phrase is played in 5th position (index finger at the 5th fret, ring finger at the 7th, etc.), except for the bends towards the end, which should be played with the ring finger jumping up to the B string's 10th fret.

## "My Friend of Misery" Interlude from *Metallica*

TRACK 59

♩ = 120

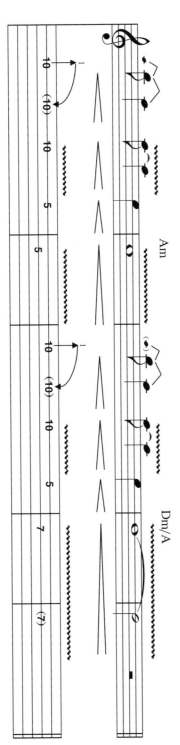

*Swell w/ vol. knob using R.H. pinky.

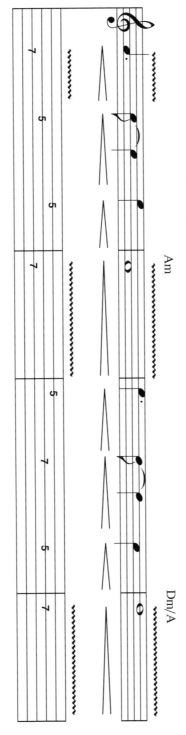

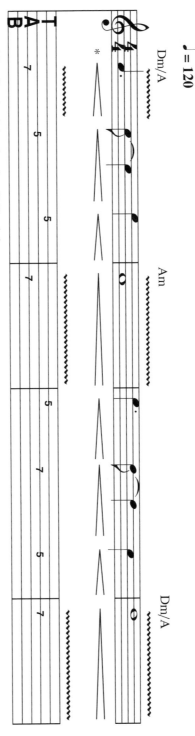

## Pinch Harmonics

This is a quintessential rock guitar technique that takes a little work to master, but it can become a mainstay of your style once you get it down. Notes are fretted normally (unlike with natural harmonics), and your picking hand does the work of producing harmonic tones above a fretted pitch. Choke up on your pick so that only the smallest amount is showing between your thumb and forefinger, and then strike the string with the pick and a little bit of either fingertip to produce the effect. The more distortion and/or volume you're working with, the easier it is to produce harmonics that really scream and slice through a rhythm section with ease. The specific pitch of the harmonic is not always indicated (and not always important), but it can be manipulated by striking the string at various distances from your guitar's bridge. Try using this technique while repeatedly striking the open G string and moving your picking hand back and forth between the end of the neck and the bridge—you'll hear a wide spectrum of harmonic tones if you're doing it correctly.

Let's look at a few examples from Metallica. The first, from "Through the Never," includes a simple B minor pentatonic (B–D–E–F#–A) lick in 7th position. Play the three whole step bend-and-releases with your ring finger while applying the pick-and-fingertip approach described above to produce harmonics two octaves above the fretted pitch. Don't worry if you're not sure about the exact harmonic produced, and remember that if you crank the volume and overdrive the harmonics will really jump out at you.

# "Through the Never" Solo from *Metallica*

**TRACK 60**

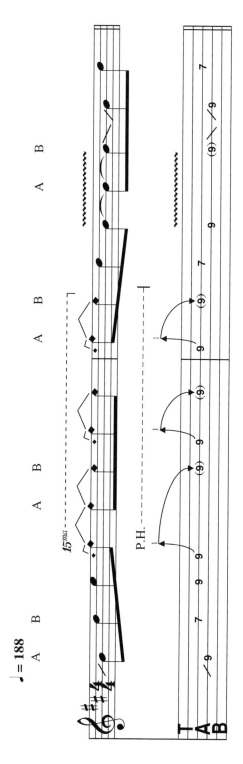

Words and Music by James Hetfield, Lars Ulrich and Kirk Hammett
Copyright © 1991 Creeping Death Music (ASCAP)
International Copyright Secured   All Rights Reserved

Here's a lick from "The Struggle Within" that's played in 3rd position and includes notes from the G minor pentatonic scale (G–B♭–C–D–F). Begin by using your ring finger to bend the D string up a quarter step, and then pull off to the open string; the second time you execute this maneuver, apply the "choke" technique to create the harmonic indicated. Two more artificial harmonics are created on the B♭ at the G string's 3rd fret; Hammett makes these emerge from his guitar as A♭s. Experiment a bit and see if you can match this pitch, but don't tear your hair out doing it. Every guitar is different and not all will respond in the same way to attempts to create specific artificial harmonic pitches.

## "The Struggle Within" Solo from *Metallica*

Words and Music by James Hetfield and Lars Ulrich
Copyright © 1991 Creeping Death Music (ASCAP)
International Copyright Secured  All Rights Reserved

TRACK 61

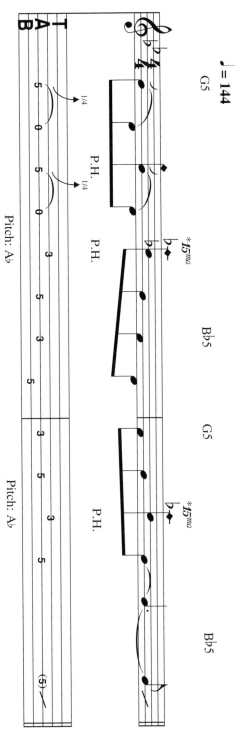

*15ma refers to harmonics only.

The lick below, from "Of Wolf and Man," features repeated pull-offs on the G, D, and A strings and includes notes from the E Dorian mode (E–F#–G–A–B–C#–D). About midway through the lick, create the indicated artificial harmonics on the G string without altering your fretting hand approach. The harmonic pitch, F#, is a perfect 5th above the fretted note, B, and should be easier to create than the flatted 7th interval in the previous example.

# "Of Wolf and Man" Solo from *Metallica*

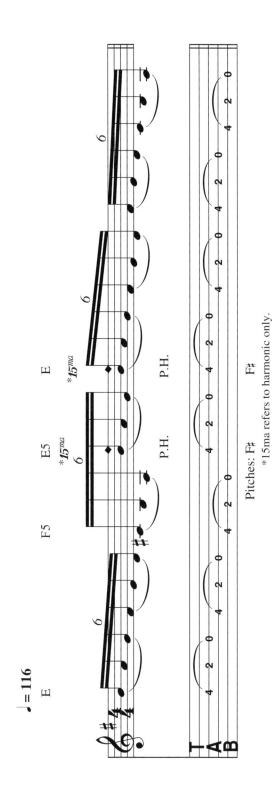

This technique involves alternate picking a given note, chord, or series of tones as quickly as possible, continuously, for the duration indicated. Think of mandolins playing the main theme from *The Godfather* and you'll get the idea. Now, anytime we hear the words "as fast as possible" on the guitar, we tend to go a little nuts, but this has to be a kind of controlled speed. The fretted notes must obey the rhythms indicated on the page, and unused strings have to be avoided so that the whole process doesn't turn into a noisy mess. Let's look at two examples.

First up is an excerpt from "Wherever I May Roam" that includes tremolo-picked double and triple stops. Fret everything here with your index finger, sliding up from one note to the next. Don't pick the final chord at the 19th fret—merely stop picking at the end of the first measure and slide on up. Remember, this should be fast *and* controlled!

## "Wherever I May Roam" Solo from *Metallica*

TRACK 63

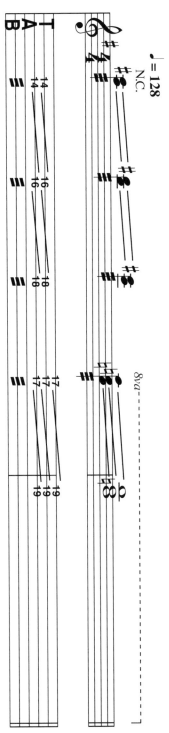

## "The Call of Ktulu" Ending from *Ride the Lightning*

Here's one from "The Call of Ktulu" that features tremolo-picked single notes on the low E string. Use the same picking hand technique as before, with rapid-fire alternate picking, while avoiding the open A string. Use your index finger to fret all of the notes on the low E string, sliding from one to another as indicated as you work your way up the neck.

TRACK 64

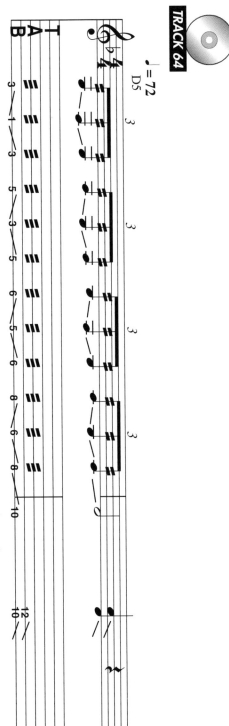

## Tapping

This advanced technique involves using a picking-hand finger to hammer on a specific pitch on the fingerboard, usually above what the fretting hand is doing. Frequently, the hammering of the picking hand is augmented by simultaneously pulling down and off the fingerboard to sound a note played by the fretting hand below. Let's look at a few licks that employ this interesting approach.

In this lick from "The Call of Ktulu," Hammett repeatedly bends the G string up a whole step with his ring finger. After the first bend, he uses his picking hand middle finger to tap the fingerboard at the 14th, 15th, and 17th frets to create grace notes that pull off into the 7th fret bend. Remember that grace notes take up no "actual" time and that immediately after pulling down and off the string with your fretting hand, you should begin the whole step bend. The final tap coincides with a pre-bend, so you should pull off with your tapping finger and bend simultaneously before slowly letting the string return to its original, unbent position.

## "The Call of Ktulu" Solo from *Ride the Lightning*

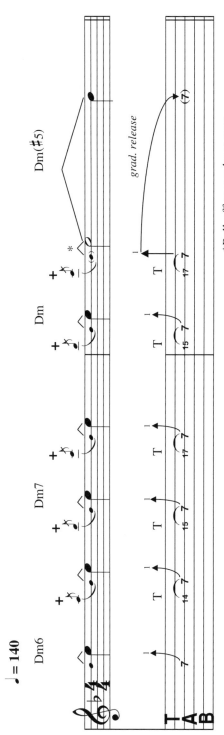

*Pull off to pre-bent note.

Words and Music by James Hetfield, Lars Ulrich, Clifford Burton and David Mustaine
Copyright © 1984 Creeping Death Music (ASCAP)
International Copyright Secured   All Rights Reserved

This lick from "Wherever I May Roam," keeps the exotic flavor of the song—set by a sitar intro—going by layering the A harmonic minor scale (A–B–C–D–E–F–G♯) over an E5 chord base. This time, Hammett uses the edge of his pick rather than a finger to tap the high E string at the 17th fret and pull off to his fretting fingers. Use your index finger at the 12th fret, your middle finger at the 13th, and your pinky at the 16th. Proceed slowly, as this one is tricky, and the difference in pull-off strength between the pick, pinky, and middle finger is very noticeable. Only by playing a lick like this over and over again at a slow speed will you be able to build up a sense of balance between the tapping and fretting fingers.

## "Wherever I May Roam" Solo from Metallica

TRACK 66

♩= 128
**Half-time feel**

*Tap w/ edge of pick.

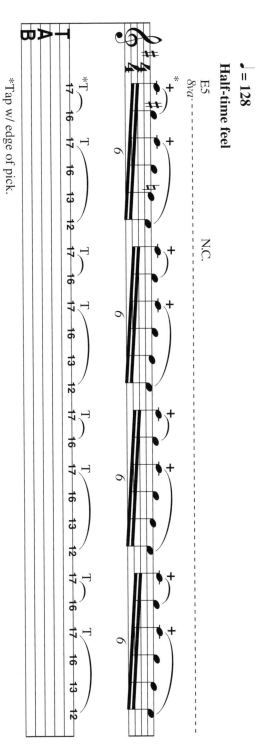

Words and Music by James Hetfield and Lars Ulrich
Copyright © 1991 Creeping Death Music (ASCAP)
International Copyright Secured  All Rights Reserved

Finally, let's take a look at a lick from "Dyers Eve" that features more tapping on the high E string. Here, Hammett plays repeated E minor triads by tapping with his middle finger on the 19th fret, and then pulls off to his ring finger at the 15th fret and index finger at the 12th. Observe the rhythms on the page and don't make these into 16th note triplets until they're indicated. The lick ends with a slide up the high E string to the 22nd fret—strike the string just once here and bend up and down with your ring finger or pinky.

# "Dyers Eve" Solo from ...And Justice for All

**TRACK 67**

♩ = 102
**Half-time feel**

Words and Music by James Hetfield, Lars Ulrich and Kirk Hammett
Copyright © 1988 Creeping Death Music (ASCAP)
International Copyright Secured   All Rights Reserved

# CHAPTER 10

## Soloing

In this final chapter, we'll analyze and learn four entire solos by Kirk Hammett that put your new techniques into practice. You'll also get an idea of how to string together licks and other melodic ideas into a coherent solo, starting with "Nothing Else Matters," which is a model of economy *and* emotion.

Learning in music happens on a number of levels. The first of these is understanding, in both theoretical and fingerboard terms—emulating great soloists is an excellent first step towards becoming one yourself, but you must understand what they're doing. Analyze each solo in this chapter and be sure that you know how the notes chosen relate to the chords over which they're played (e.g., an F# is the 9th of an E chord, but it's a raised 11th when played over a C chord). Be sure you understand the rhythms and how they work against the basic pulse. Scales and modes are also crucial; they make up the raw material from which a solo is constructed. The next level of understanding is the technical one—how do I play this on the guitar? This means fingering choices, hand positioning, and picking. Then comes the struggle to get the music under your fingers and up to tempo so you can play it convincingly. Finally, there is assimilation, in which the music you've learned becomes a part of you so deeply that it can be used to help build your own, original solo style.

The brief, 11-measure passage below from "Nothing Else Matters" manages to be both melodic and blisteringly heated while unfolding gradually to an intense climax. The harmonic backdrop provided by the band is squarely in E minor, so the E minor pentatonic scale (E–G–A–B–D) and E Dorian mode (E–F#–G–A–B–C#–D) are used while staying mostly within 12th position.

Begin the solo with your pinky on the B string (15th fret) and your ring finger bending and then releasing the G string. At the end of this measure, you leave 12th position briefly and move your index finger down to the 11th fret for the Dorian mode phrase in measure 2. The third measure includes a typical blues-rock bending phrase as well as a few *blue notes*—the ♭5 added to the standard pentatonic scale (here, B♭). Measure 4 begins with an index-finger bend on the G string that's followed by some descending double stops, while measure 5 finds you sliding up the high E string to the 17th fret with the pinky before sliding back down in measure 6. Measure 7 represents the climactic moment in the solo and is made up entirely of ideas that appeared in the previous measures. This is particularly instructive, in that Hammett knows that re-use of material serves to unify a musical statement and add cohesion and structural integrity. Don't ignore the lesson—when you hit upon something good, don't just throw it away after playing it once!

## "Nothing Else Matters" Solo from *Metallica*

TRACK 68

♩. = 46

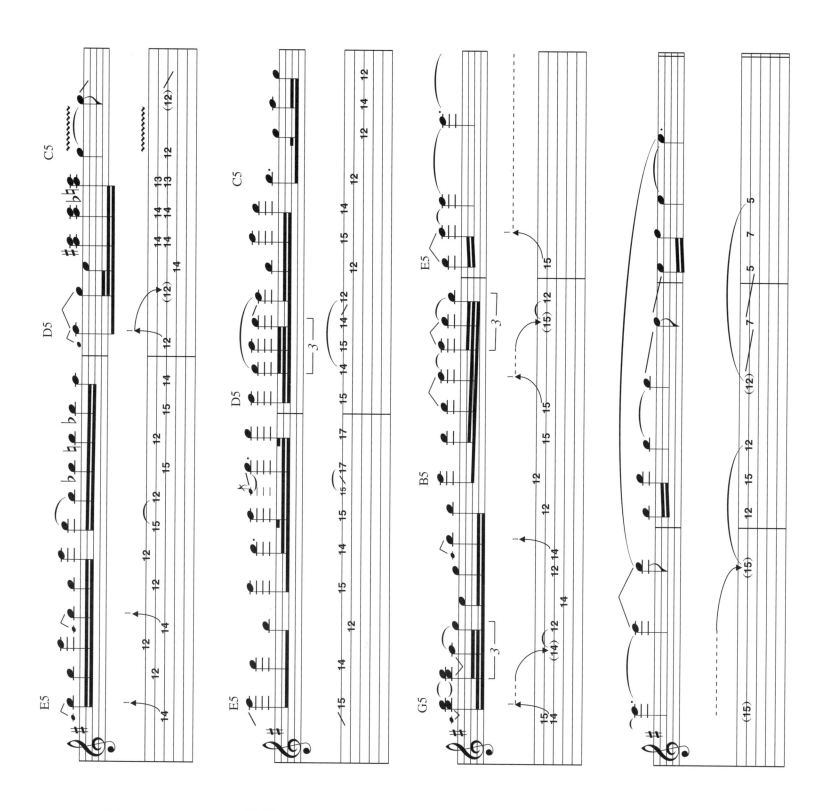

Next up is a longer solo from "Through the Never." Hammett begins in the stratosphere, with four measures played in 19th position, with the B minor pentatonic scale (B–D–E–F♯–A) an octave higher than its usual 7th fret address. The licks here aren't particularly hard, but they can be if you're not used to playing this high up on the neck where your fretting fingers have limited space in which to move around. By now, you know the drill—take it very slowly, repeating the licks over and over again until you can maneuver satisfactorily in such close quarters. In measure 5, he slides down the neck to 7th position, making things easier for a while. You should recognize most of the licks that follow from our discussions of artificial harmonics, double stops, and string bending found earlier in this book. Jump ahead to measure 17 and up to 17th position for the four-measure stretch where Hammett uses notes from the A minor pentatonic scale (A–C–D–E–G) an octave higher than their usual 5th fret setting. The step-and-a-half over-bends in measures 19 and 20 should be played with the ring finger, with the index and middle fingers assisting, unless your pinky is exceptionally strong.

## "Through the Never" Solo from *Metallica*

TRACK 69

♩ = 188

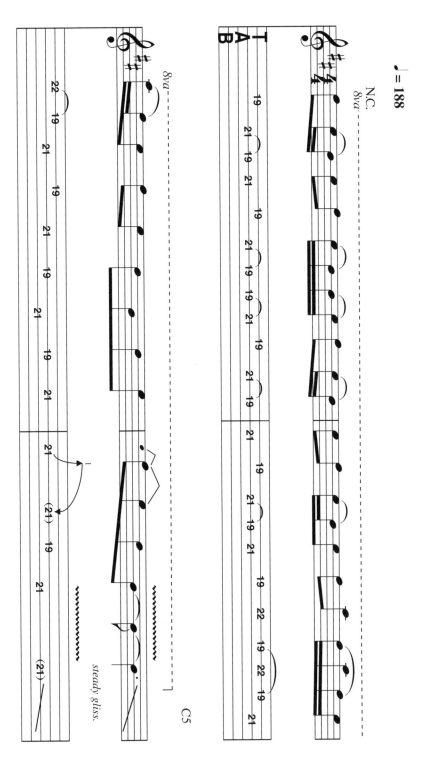

Words and Music by James Hetfield, Lars Ulrich and Kirk Hammett
Copyright © 1991 Creeping Death Music (ASCAP)
International Copyright Secured   All Rights Reserved

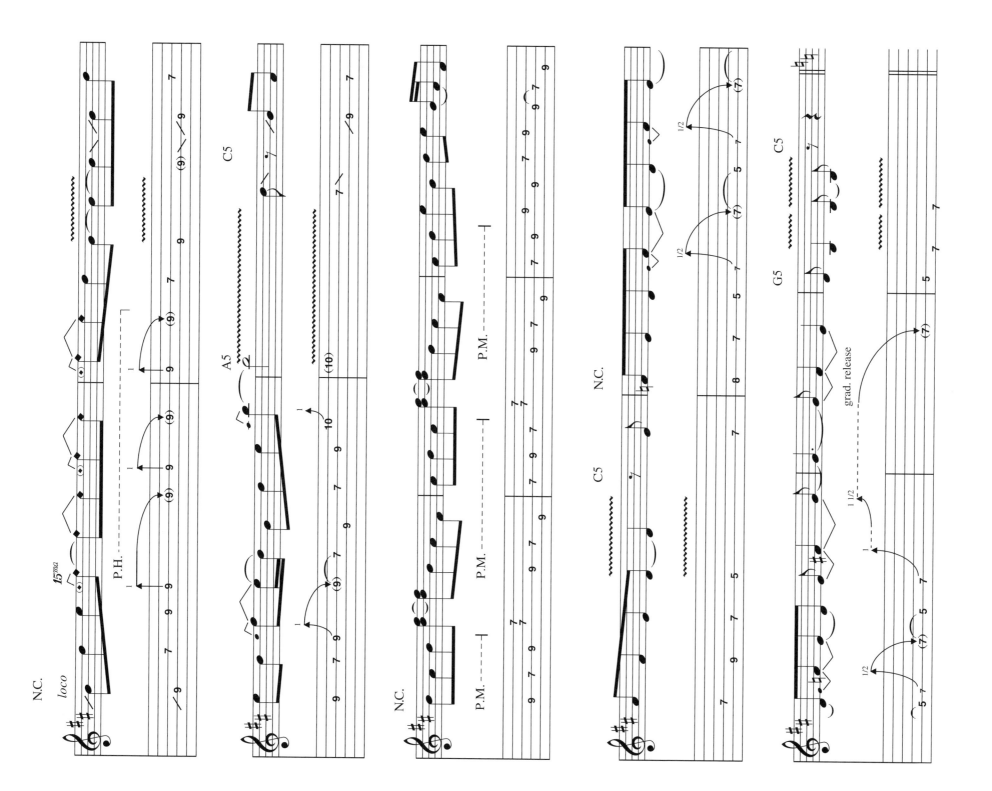

The ridiculously heavy "Sad but True" includes both a ten-measure solo (shown here with the 11th measure that bleeds over into the vocal's return) and a second five-measure solo shortly after. Let's look at the shorter (and easier) one first. Remember to tune down a whole step if you're going to play along with the recording.

Hammett begins his second solo in open position, playing a handful of licks that absolutely confirm his identity as a bluesman in headbanger's clothing. Use your middle finger for all 2nd-fret notes and bends, and your ring finger to execute the 3rd-fret notes in measure 2. The marriage of bent and open strings is textbook blues guitar, tuned down and cranked way the hell up. Return to your ring finger for the measure 3 step-and-a-half overbends and add a little bit of finger to the string with your picking hand to produce the semi-harmonics indicated on the page. The solo wraps up with a climb to the 12th-position box and some repeated double stops and familiar bending licks.

# "Sad but True" Solo II from *Metallica*

TRACK 70

Tune down 1 step:
(low to high) D-G-C-F-A-D

Words and Music by James Hetfield and Lars Ulrich
Copyright © 1991 Creeping Death Music (ASCAP)
International Copyright Secured  All Rights Reserved

## "Sad but True" Solo I from *Metallica*

This final example takes us back in the song to Hammett's longer "Sad but True" solo. Start with the sliding double stops examined earlier in the section detailing that technique (index finger on the B string; middle finger on the G string). After some typical 12th-position pentatonic licks, there's an interesting phrase in measures 3 and 4 that begins with a pull-off at the 9th fret of the G string from the pinky to the middle and index fingers. Play the grace-note slide up to B (and subsequent slide down the D string) at the end of measure 3 with your middle finger. Start measure 4 with your index finger and you'll be in proper position to complete the phrase. Notice how Hammett uses both C and C♯ in the same lick—a shift from the E Aeolian mode (E–F♯–G–A–B–C–D) to the E Dorian (E–F♯–G–A–B–C♯–D) mode that we've seen more frequently in previous examples. As the solo progresses, he continues to swing back and forth between modes. After some blazing pentatonic licks in measures 5 and 6 (slow 'em down—waaaay down), Hammett spends the next two measures bending a 14th-fret double stop up and down with his ring finger, giving the E Dorian mode's signature C♯ (a major 6th against a minor chord) a place of prominence. The solo climaxes with an ascending lick made up of a series of sextuplets that shifts from the E minor pentatonic scale to the E Aeolian mode with the introduction of the C♮ towards the end of measure 9. Stay in 12th position until the third beat of measure 11 and you shouldn't find the going too tough. On that third beat, however, shift up ever so slightly so that the Cs on the B string's 13th fret are played with the index finger. This allows you to execute the final bends with your ring finger, the pinky anchoring the high E string at the 15th fret above. Obviously, learning a solo like this (or any other tough material) really underscores the importance of proper fingering—without it, you're fighting a losing battle. Good Luck!

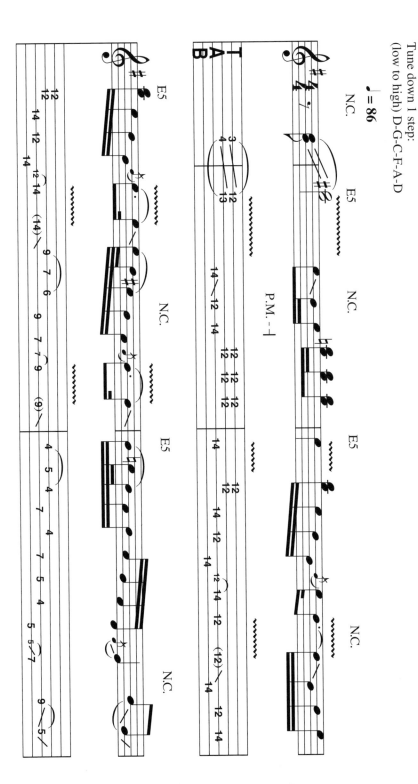

Tune down 1 step:
(low to high) D-G-C-F-A-D

♩ = 86

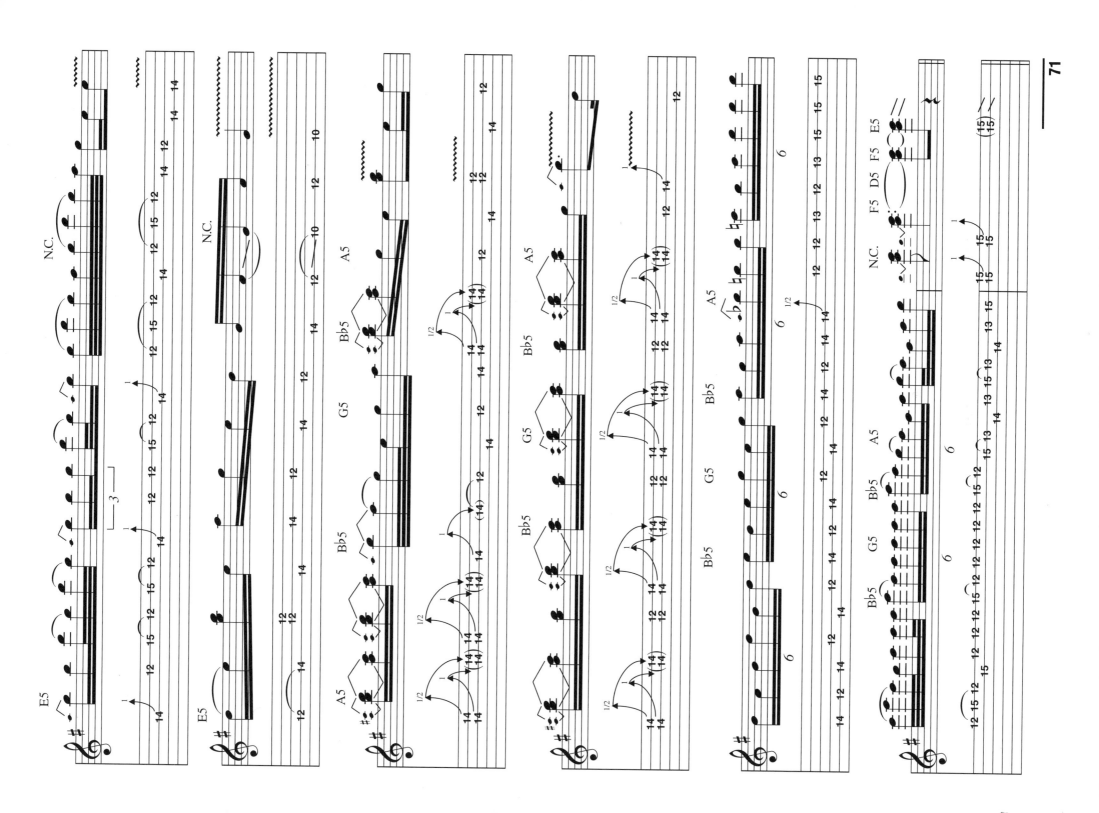